Water Balloon

Water Balloon

Audrey Vernick

Houghton Mifflin Harcourt
New York | Boston

All rights reserved. Originally published in hardcover
in the United States by Harcourt Children's Books,
an imprint of Houghton Mifflin Harcourt Publishing Company, 2011.

For information about permission to reproduce selections from this book,
write to Permissions, Houghton Mifflin Harcourt Publishing Company,
215 Park Avenue South, New York, New York 10003.

www.hmhco.com

The text of this book is set in Horley Old Style MT.

The Library of Congress has cataloged the hardcover edition as follows:
Vernick, Audrey.
Water balloon/Audrey Vernick.
p. cm.
[1. Fathers and daughters—Fiction. 2. Babysitting—Fiction.
3. Best friends—Fiction. 4. Friendship—Fiction. 5. Dogs—Fiction.
6. Divorce—Fiction.]
I. Title.
PZ7.V5973Wat 2011
811'.54—dc22   2005024610

ISBN: 978-0-547-59554-2 hardcover
ISBN: 978-0-544-27501-0 paperback

Manufactured in the United States of America
DOC 10 9 8 7 6 5 4 3 2 1

For my best friends,
Ellen Gidaro and Beth Arnold,
who happen, by the best good fortune,
to also be my sisters

Brightly Colored Happiness

∞

The blitzing began five years ago, in second grade, on one of those amazing spring days that remind you how hot summer can be. I was sitting outside, waiting for my best friends to come over. I knew we'd spend the day outside—the weather was the kind of gorgeous that makes you feel stupid if you spend a minute indoors.

I have no idea why I had a bag of balloons in the garage, but I did. Before Leah and Jane arrived, I blew up a ton with the hose and filled this big planter behind my dad's grill with water balloons.

Whenever we hung out, we played Monopoly. We were inventing our own rules, our own way to play. Whoever bought Park Place had to get drinks for all players. If you landed on Marvin Gardens, the other players had to quickly come up with a new hairstyle for you. That kind of thing. These days, there's an action associated with every space. (Except Baltic. If you land on Baltic, you can just relax.) But on that day, we were still making it up.

So there we were, playing our evolving version of Monopoly on the wooden picnic table in the backyard. Leah was leaning back to get some sun on her face. Jane was focused on the game, like me. She had a pad next to her, keeping track of the random action we applied to each space.

I landed on B&O Railroad, which, according to our rules, meant I had to go get pretzels for them. Instead, I went to the planter.

Was there a minute, a pause, before I started throwing the balloons? A second when I realized that something way beyond awesome was about to take place? I wish I could remember.

What I do remember is the identical look on their faces. I managed to hit Jane and Leah within seconds of each other, and it was as if they had no idea what had happened. Did the sky just fall? Did a bird crap on them? Did their heads explode? How could they suddenly be wet, sitting outside on a hot spring day? Almost before it was humanly possible, they were right there beside me, pulling balloons out and attacking me right back. There was water everywhere, wet everything, balloons flying, breaking apart, arms throwing and trying to deflect, voices squealing, screaming, laughing. We were running, trying to get away, running back, getting more balloons from the planter. It was wet and brightly colored happiness of the splatted, splattered water balloon variety.

Rig raced out barking, running circles around us. My parents ran out of the house too; all the noise must have set off their Parent Alerts. Mom and Dad took it all in: how wet we were, how hard we were laughing, the red and yellow and blue and purple balloon splats everywhere. Instead of yelling at us to clean it all up, or did we realize we had nearly drenched a perfectly good Monopoly game, or even *What the hell is going on out here?,* my mom found one balloon that had landed unbroken and smashed it directly on my dad's head.

She looked so happy! Almost proud, in a goofy way. Dad had that look of wonder he always got—as if he couldn't believe how great she was. Or how lucky he was. A look I haven't seen in so long.

First Water Balloon Blitz. Quite possibly the best water balloon fight in the history of mankind.

* * *

The next year, Jane ambushed Leah and me at the park. She had her brother and father help her hide a stash in this big bin behind the playground, and she just totally blindsided us with a water balloon attack of pure excellence.

What impressed me most was not the total shock factor, or the way Jane made an annual tradition out of what we all had thought of as the greatest ever onetime event. I just loved the *Jane way* she went about it. It was so well planned. I mean, she brought the full water balloons to the park in a bucket half filled with water so they wouldn't break. Seriously—that was taking it to a whole other level.

Over the years, rules evolved. We came up with a points system.

The Water Balloon Blitz can only be after school ends, and there can be only one blitz per year. Points are given in the following categories:

Number of witnesses to water balloon blitzing.

Number of days since last day of school—in other words, the longer you wait, the more points you get. Of course, there's also a greater the chance of someone else bombing you first.

Bonus points for courage—it's a lot easier to launch a surprise balloon attack on your best friends when it's just the three of you in a backyard than it is in a public place or when your friend's parents might kill you.

Which is why Leah is reigning champion. Her attack at Jane's sister's birthday party two years ago was a thing of great beauty. And utter surprise. Leah wasn't exactly a follower, but she sure wasn't a leader. She mostly went along with what Jane and I did. So for her to come up with this blitz, this most incredibly courageous blitz, well, Jane and I were nearly speechless for days. And Leah was never the same herself.

All these older neighbors were there, not to mention Jane's mega-uptight mother and grandmother, but Leah went all out, bombing Jane and me. Most of the other guests, too. Jane and I kneeled down before her at the end of that party. Literally.

The weird thing is that last summer, there was no blitz. All through August, I was sure I'd score with a ton of points by waiting so long, but the days slipped by, and Jane and Leah were so busy all the time. I never blitzed them. They never blitzed me. Then seventh grade started. And life went on.

Well, life didn't exactly go on. My life got a little stopped for a while. Or it felt like it did, when Dad moved out.

I'm in Danger, People

As we take the last turn to my dad's new place, the car's headlights swoop up a sloping lawn. Caught for an instant, shining in that light, is a patch of ghostly dandelions, puffy silver heads aglow, like phantom flowers.

"Hunh!" Mom says. I know what she means. My dad is some kind of weed freak. When we all lived together back home, the minute a weed even thought about starting to grow, Dad would be there in his grungy gardening clothes with a shovel and this complicated tool he built to make sure he gets all the roots when he digs it out. I'm thinking that maybe we're at the wrong place, but Mom pulls right into the driveway and gets out of the car. "Come on, Marley," she says. I check my pocket for my phone—the only way I could feel more stranded this summer would be if my mother drove off with my phone. Okay. Got it. We each take a bag from the trunk.

"Let's go, Rig," I say into the back seat, and he scrambles up to all fours. God, I love my dog. If a movie director said, "Quick! Get me a black shaggy mutt!," a dog that looked just like Rig would come trotting into the studio.

He looks out the window, then looks at me, wondering.

I'm wondering too.

* * *

Inside, Mom and Dad stand half a room apart, being all polite to each other. I can't help it. I still hope that Mom will laugh until she makes that high-pitched noise that sounds like a held-in sneeze and then put up her hand, begging him to stop whatever he's saying. Or that Dad will look at her with half a smile while almost shaking his head, the look that means he loves her.

But Dad's just pointing his index finger toward another room. "Can I get you a drink?" he asks.

"Oh, no, no," Mom says, like she's talking to someone she hardly knows.

They've been living apart for four months now. I've seen my dad almost every Sunday and at least one school night every week. But not since he got settled in this new place last week. Everything keeps changing—my family, where my dad lives, where I sleep. I want to squeeze the brakes tight and screech to a stop.

"Really, I should get going," Mom says. "I want to hit the road early." Not long after Dad moved out, Mom discovered Facebook. Every day she was talking about reconnecting with some long-lost friend from elementary school or high school or camp. (Who knew she went to camp?) And now she's taking her very own Facebook road trip, visiting with all these people she hasn't seen in decades. Then she's going to help my grandmother while she recovers from some kind of surgery on her hip.

She goes over some lists and phone numbers with him and all of a sudden I'm thinking, *Oh, no. No. I don't think so! Mom! You can't leave me here.* Dad is funny and smart and he loves me a lot. But he's more like some kind of Marley spectator than any kind of parenting parent. He's like a devoted fan. Mom knows how my life works. As she starts to gather her stuff together, I feel like screaming. *I can't live here with him!*

This has been planned for so long now that it seems to have a forward-moving motion all its own. I'm to stay with Dad for all of July and most of August too. I'll have a couple of weeks with Mom before I go back to school.

She hugs me tight and I squeeze my eyes shut to keep the tears from spilling out. I've never been great at goodbyes. I was the one, Mom always says, hugging her leg tight each morning, keeping her from walking out the heavy wooden door of Little Ones Nursery School. She's the director of a preschool herself and she says there's always one kid who clings. That was me. I still remember how much it hurt to be apart from my mother back then—like a big raw hole inside me. I guess not that much has changed; I want to wrap myself around her leg right now.

Mom pats Rig's head and says she'll talk to me in a couple of days. Right. The phone. Okay. We'll talk.

* * *

Rig hasn't seen Dad in a while, but they're right back to it—the total boy way they play together, all physical and slappy. Dad pretends to hit the side of Rig's mouth; Rig makes his chimpanzee noise. Before long, they're rolling around on the floor together, and it's all just so very, very boyish.

With me, Rig's a cuddler. He's big, but he still sits in my lap when I sit on the floor. He backs into me, then slowly lowers his rear until he's sitting. He usually looks over his shoulder, as though making sure I see and appreciate his efforts.

Rig's real name is Gehrig, which was Dad's idea. I think Dad wanted a son, and I think he wanted to name *him* Gehrig.

I'm not any kind of baseball genius, but you can't be my dad's daughter without knowing that Lou Gehrig was a Yankee. A great Yankee—kind, talented, and humble. Even though he died before my dad was born, and even though he wasn't the team's biggest star, he's still Dad's favorite. He says that Lou Gehrig was one of the most gifted players ever but other great players, like Babe Ruth, always overshadowed him. With friends like Leah and Jane, I think I have a pretty good idea how Lou must have felt.

I start to think about how Rig and Dad and I are going to be spending all this time together, this big mess of time, when Dad's not out doing the gardening jobs he took on for the summer. It's the first time he's ever worked in the summer. When I picture Dad working, I see him in his teacher clothes, erasing equations and then with a sponge cleaning the entire blackboard, including every bit of chalk dust on the metal chalk rail. (I'm pretty sure he's the only teacher in his school to still use a blackboard.)

It always requires a mental adjustment when I see him in sunshine, or even in short sleeves. But if ever there was a man meant to take care of lawns, it's my dad.

He waves his hand in front of my face. "Are you listening?" he asks.

I give my head a quick shake, a little like a dog myself, and look at him.

"I *said*," he starts, all put out, "you'll be babysitting during the week, from the morning until sometime after lunch."

"What? When? For who?"

"When? The summer."

"You mean more than one day?"

"I mean more than one day. Yes. For the summer. While you're here. I worked it out so you'll have a place to be while I'm working," he says.

"I thought I'd just be hanging out."

He makes his cough sound of annoyance. It's all air,

no throat. "We talked about this. I asked if you'd be interested in babysitting and you said you would."

"What?! I meant like once or twice. Not—You mean every *day?*"

"Yes. I mean every day. Well, not weekends, of course."

"Can't I just hang out? Or help you at your jobs?"

"I've already promised Lynne Kroll that you'll do this."

"I can't believe this. I don't even know a Lynne Kroll!" I'm getting louder. I take a deep breath and stop. It's almost like anger doesn't exist in our family. If I yell or stomp, Dad throws up his hands like a disgusted old man with no patience for the young. I lift the hair up off my neck. When did I start sweating?

He's just sitting on his couch, watching me, waiting for me to catch up, to get past this bit of disbelief, to accept. Usually I do, but this is crazy. Am I some kind of servant, some no-vote-permitted, do-as-you're-told little-kid servant? *Think!* "I thought this summer was all about living with you. Why can't I just help you out on your jobs? We could spend more time together that way."

He straightens newspapers on the coffee table, no longer even looking at me. "I have to give the appearance of being professional; these people don't want teenage girls lounging on their lawns, Marley. It's not a good place for you—I use saws and dangerous tools. It wouldn't work out."

I would like to point out that if I'm old enough to be in charge of someone's stupid kid, I can probably handle being near a lawn mower.

He looks at my face and something in his own softens. "Marley, I promised Lynne you'd help her. She's counting on you. It will be fine. You'll make money—I'm sure you could use some money—and you'll probably love what you're doing. It'll be great."

For you, I think. *Great for you.*

*　＊　＊　＊*

I stomp into the bedroom to call Jane.

"When do you start?" Jane asks. "That's so lame. I can't believe your dad would do that. I thought your parents were cool."

"I'm supposed to start on Monday. I can't believe this. It's so not right."

"I wish you could come with Leah and me to Curtain Call."

"Because that's so me?"

"It would be better than babysitting."

"Being with you guys, yeah, definitely. But you know I can't act. I don't want to act. I'd rather . . ."

"What?"

"I don't know . . . anything? I mean, I think what you do is amazing," I say. "Your version of *Cinderella* in sixth grade was the funniest thing I ever saw in my life."

"CinderELLA! CinderELLA! Go get my dress! CinderELLA! CinderELLA! Fix my hair."

"You know, maybe I *should* just see if my dad would pay for me to—"

"Actually, I don't think there are any spots left in our division. I'm pretty sure Leah said she got the last one. I'm sorry. Did you really want to—"

"I'm just desperate, no. I don't think I would. Ugh."

"Ugh is right."

"So are you and Leah coming over tomorrow?"

"Yeah, after orientation, okay?"

"You have orientation on a Sunday?"

"Just a quick thing in the morning. We'll be there sometime in the afternoon."

"Cool. Then whose house for the Fourth this year?"

"We'll figure it out tomorrow. I'll see ya, Marley."

* * *

When I wake up in the morning, I have that freaky pat-the-blankets, look-at-the-walls moment. Where am I? My room does not have light blue walls. The sun does not filter in beneath my window shade and shine directly on my head. Rig arches his belly up toward the ceiling, his paws stretching straight out. Rig, with his steady eyes. Rig with me here. Where? Right. Dad's.

I walk into the kitchen. Actually, a little morning-groggy, I walk into both bathrooms before I find the kitchen. Dad is standing at the counter, holding a container of the wrong kind of orange juice. I hate pulp. Odd little plates are on the counter next to weird little juice cups. The odd clear-glass plates are piled high with scrambled eggs. At least he got the egg part right.

Rig's nails click into the room and Dad kneels down and starts to rub his ears. Then he looks up and sees me, and there's all this love in his eyes. Oh, my dad.

I'm such a mess. A kind look from someone—from my *dad*—and I'm ready to burst into tears. It's just everything, too much change at once. I can't even figure out—like, at all—why my parents aren't together. Watching a relationship go bad might be like watching something grow. If you're there all the time, you can't see it happening. Rig weighed only eight pounds when we got him. I could hold him in my hands. Now he's this big black mess of a dog. It was slow, bit by bit. With my parents, there must have been changes over time. They were just invisible to me. It was hard to notice because they didn't yell a lot. In the end, they didn't talk a lot, either. There was a lot of silence those last months, but it wasn't the peaceful kind. It had weight, an angry silence.

"Morning," I say. I walk over to the counter and start to move things to the table. Odd plates. Weird juice cups. Napkins.

I sit at the table and watch him butter his toast with painterly precision, up to but not including the crust. Behind him on the wall there's a clock shaped like a coffee cup. It is so weird to me that Dad lives in this place. I keep glancing back from the plates to the cups. Oh, and those forks. Where did they all come from? Were they always in this house? Did he buy them? I picture him with this empty shopping cart, setting out to buy all the things he'll need to live by himself. I see him looking at different cups and plates and putting them in his cart and then, maybe thinking of Mom and me, putting them back on the shelf, and then back in the cart again. I picture him walking slowly down a wide aisle, pushing that new-at-living-alone-dad cart.

He places his toast, perfectly centered on a plate, on

the table and goes to the fridge. "Since we're both free today," he says, his face actually in the refrigerator, "I thought we could do something fun. Something together."

I nod until he pulls his face back out and can see me. "Leah and Jane are coming over this afternoon. After Curtain Call."

"We'll be back. Did you bring a bathing suit?" He puts two unopened jars of jam on the table—strawberry and grape.

"Why?"

"I thought we'd take Rig to the lake. Maybe get a rowboat and fish for a while. Maybe you could swim, too. It should be warm enough later."

Really? Because you said something fun.

I never used to complain about fishing days back when we lived our old life, our Perfectly Good Life. Because a fishing day never had anything to do with fishing for Mom and me. We'd send Dad off with his pole and he'd fish while we did normal things. We'd talk, swim, eat. I always had a good time.

But his won't be anything like that.

This—this!—seems like a whole new world with a set of rules that no one remembered to share with me. If we were in our Perfectly Good Life, it would be a day that just happened, natural. I chew the toast, disgusted by how dry it is in my mouth.

"I'll get ready now," I say. Like a line in a play. On this strange set with these weird prop plates and little prop glasses filled with pulpy orange juice.

* * *

We pack a cooler with drinks and snacks and a container of water for Rig, then drive for a very long time, out to a lake I've never seen before.

It looks like a postcard of perfect summer. There's a dock, an area for swimming, some boats, and picnic tables painted bright white. It must be too early for normal people, because it's deserted. But then, normal people are home in bed. Or hanging out with their friends.

Okay. I just have to survive fishing. Then Leah and Jane will come over and start to make this summer bearable. I can almost see Leah, sprawled on my new bed with a magazine quiz open in front of her. Jane will have a notebook open to a page divided into three columns, our names in neat letters at the top of each, to record our answers. Okay. Who can't survive one fishing trip?

Dad loads himself up with stuff from the car— fishing poles crossed over his shoulder, container of bait in one hand, the cooler pulling down the other. I run ahead with Rig while Dad pays a guy in a little shack. We all slog through the mud to the water's edge, and I watch as Dad loads everything onto a rowboat. Rig looks around, as though he's trying to figure out what's expected of him here. Dad snaps his fingers and points at the boat and Rig splashes into the water and clambers aboard. The boat tips back wildly and Rig gets this crazy look in his eyes, this *How could you ever put me in this situation?* look, this *I'M IN DANGER, PEOPLE* look, and hoo boy, do I ever get how he feels. I grab the splintery oar, then the side of the boat itself, to still the rocking. I climb in and put a steadying hand on his neck. He thumps his tail once and sits at my feet, his chin on my left knee.

Dad fiddles with the oars and starts rowing out. There's the *shplush* sound of the oars hitting the water, then a *thluup* as they come out. Dad's looking back toward the dock we just left. I'm looking at Dad's old Yankees baseball cap, scratching Rig's ears until his left rear paw is thump, thump, thumping. Every time I rub his ears just right, his left rear paw just does that—it's some kind of reflex that signals dog bliss. *Shplush . . . thluup. Shplush . . . thluup. Thump thump thump.*

I'm waiting for the right moment. I figure maybe out here, in Dadland, I can get him to see how unfair he's being about this stupid babysitting thing. Even *he* has to be able to see that normal people do not surprise their children with unwanted jobs.

When he gets us to some place that must seem right to him (it looks like the rest of the lake to me), he stops rowing. Rig lies down in the bottom of the boat, his head readjusted to rest on my right foot. Dad digs a worm out of the container. Ew.

So this is what I've been missing when I hang out with Mom on fishing days. I watch my dad impale one creature to catch another.

He throws the line back over his shoulder and swings it into the lake. *Splish!* Then he hands me the rod to hold.

"Did you bring a radio to listen to the game?" Sports radio chatter and baseball games have been the background music of all my summers. Dad shakes his head. I don't exactly like listening to all that baseball talk, but it gives me a lot to discuss with my dad: this one's hitting streak, that one's trouble with the inside fastball.

"How's the gardening stuff going?" I ask. "Is it fun or anything?" From Dad's summer job it's just one more conversational step to the babysitting thing. I can do this. I'm almost there.

"We can't talk, Marley." He points down. Huh? Is

there some new way Dad and I are supposed to communicate now that he doesn't live with Mom and me? He sucks in his lips and crosses his eyes. Is he dying? Has he lost his mind? He points out at our lines, just sitting in the water. I still don't get it. Finally, exasperated, he says, "The fish."

Oh. Duh. The fish. But . . . but, but, but! *Dad! Are you at all sorry about making me do a job I don't want? Have you missed me? Do you wonder if maybe someday things might get back to our Perfectly Good Life? Do you ever think about Mom?*

I look out at my line, unmoving in the still waters. So this is it? Fishing is about silently holding something? Wow.

I wonder when the Curtain Call orientation will end, how much longer until I'm finally hanging with my friends again. I wonder if Leah will like it. Jane's been going since she was six, but Leah always used to spend a ton of time visiting her grandmother on Cape Cod, so she never signed up for Curtain Call before.

I bet she'll love it.

Leah and Jane spent almost all of seventh grade in drama club together. They were so into it at the end of the year, with all the extra rehearsals and performances and cast parties, that I hardly ever saw them. Acting might not be my thing, but it's clearly theirs.

Much to my guidance counselor's obvious disappointment, the things I like to do, other than just hang with my friends, are kind of solitary things, like reading and writing and doodling. I was the poetry editor of the school's literary magazine (creatively named the *LitMag*) with this amazing writer, Callie, who was fiction editor. The issue we put out at the end of the year was kind of incredible and intense, but really, I'd rather not be part of the *LitMag* at all. I think I'm just not an organized activities kind of girl. There's this unspoken rule, though, that you have to do *something*.

There must have been a bunch of kids in our school who didn't, but when I try to think of them, the only one I can picture is Elsie Jenkins, this über-pale girl who wears a tan windbreaker year-round. It's an outer garment in the spring and fall and an extra layer indoors during the winter. Elsie, as Jane once pointed out, is monochromatic. Her hair and her face are all this washed out, unnameable color, a hue that blends right into the windbreaker. I don't think she has ever had a friend. As far as I know, she has never joined a club. I've only heard her speak once, when she asked me something about submitting a poem for the literary magazine. She never did, though. She's quiet and kind of painful.

Why am I thinking about Elsie Jenkins, tan-windbreaker loner girl? Could it be because I'm sitting on a boat, participating in the silent holding of a fishing rod with my dad, my who-cares-what-Marley-wants-to-do dad, with no friends in sight for what feels like fourteen hours?

There has never, in the history of modern civilization, been a morning with more time in it.

I don't catch anything.

By the time we're done, Dad catches two fish. He throws them back.

Yeah, that was worthwhile.

I think about an endless span of days, of living with Dad and the monotony of watching some little kid. A whole summer of days as long and boring as this one. I want to jump into the lake and swim away, swim into a perfect summer.

Shouldn't I Be Licensed for This Kind of Work?

W hen we get back to Dad's, I let him unload everything from the truck into his garage and I run into the house. I feel all fishy and I want to shower before Leah and Jane get here.

I'm about to call Jane to find out what time they're coming, but there's a message from Leah. "Marley? Listen, I'm really sorry, but I don't think we're going to be able to come over today. OH! My God. We got all this prep work we have to do before the first class. I didn't know there'd be, like, *homework*. Anyway, we're working in groups, and Jane and me—listen, I'll just call you later and explain, okay? I hope you're having fun."

Oh, yes. I'm having a great time. Woo. Hoo.

I call Mom's cell phone. She has to fix this. I don't care if she's on a mini-vacation, visiting with friends or whatever. She has to make this better. I leave a message, ask her to call me as soon as she can.

Dad calls in from the garage, "A little help?" I go in the bathroom, pretend I didn't hear him. Wasn't fishing his idea? Let him put away all his own stuff in his own stupid way. There's never been a more this-goes-here-and-that-goes-there kind of person than Robert Baird.

After my shower, I can't find a place for myself. At home, I have my spots—the throw rug on my bedroom floor, my chair at the kitchen table, the love seat in the den. I take my book and try the living room couch. It's kind of hard, not inviting. I sit on a stool at the kitchen counter and open my book, but after two pages, I'm up and looking for a new spot, feeling a little Goldilocks-y.

"Hey, Marley," my dad calls from his room. "I need to go through some of these boxes. Would you give me a hand?"

I walk out the kitchen door into the backyard. I head through the weedy grass and sit under a big tree toward the back with my book until it gets too dark to read. I'm not entirely proud of myself.

* * *

The next morning I'm up very early, and I have that same confused feeling of wondering where I am, and then there's Rig, with his big head just resting on my bed. My bed at Dad's.

Why didn't Mom call back last night? Now I'm stuck for today. I have to babysit.

And Leah never called back.

Jane didn't call.

Yay.

Rig leads me to the door. At home, there's a back door that I think of as Rig's door. When he has to go out, he sits there, patiently. When we're not in the room, he stands there, and he has this very soft, I-don't-mean-to-be-rude-or-interrupt "Ruh" he uses to get our attention. His language is all *Ruh* all the time, but it's always been clear to me what he's trying to say. I am fluent in Rigspeak. Poor Rig! We haven't even taken the time to show him what to do here. He doesn't know where to "Ruh."

"Hang on a sec," I whisper to him. He looks at me, then sits.

On top of my little duffle bag, Dad left me a new shirt last night, a present. A Yankees shirt. I recognize this—it's a gesture. It's how my family speaks. Dad is telling me something. It means something like *I know I do things that drive you crazy, but I'm glad you're here.* I'm about to dig out something more normal when Rig whimpers, reminding me that he's waiting, that a doggy bladder cannot just pass the time while a frivolous girl seeks out suitably cool clothes. I reach into the big duffle and pull out shorts and pull them on along with the navy blue shirt with the white entwined *NY.*

I lead Rig through the kitchen and out the back door. He's the kind of dog that would never take off, even if a gang of gorgeous golden retrievers was strolling down the street with trays of bacon strapped on their backs. So I let him explore, and I look around. The grass is still dewy this early, but what is really amazing are the clumps of dandelions. Usually there aren't so many this time of year. For whatever reason, there are dandelions at all different stages of life—yellow flowers, puffy white globes, some closed tight, others looking ready to spread their seed at the first wind—in small clusters all over the lawn.

When people describe flowers, they use lovely adjectives—*delicate, fragrant, elegant*. A dandelion is its own thing: bright and resilient. I start to gather the yellow ones, collecting a bouquet. I try to pull them out the way Dad taught me to, reaching down deep for the roots, but they break at the stem.

Sometimes I imagine a different world where people love dandelions and jump up and down, slapping high-fives with their neighbors each time one shows up. They'd be reeling from the wonder of it all—this cheerful yellow bud that just appears without even having to plant it. (What? It's a fantasy. Are all your fantasies totally normal?)

Rig, on the other side of the bushes, lets out a single "Ruh." It sounds like his *Hi, friend* bark, louder than his *I have to pee* bark, somehow friendlier. I wonder if he's found a new squirrel friend. He's quiet after the one "Ruh," so I turn my attention back to the lawn.

I walk all over and find some long grasses and goldenrod and a few little white clover flowers. I line the dandelions in a neat row and trim the bottoms with my fingernails so they're even. I tuck goldenrod and clover between the stems, wrap the grass around the bundle three times, then tie a perfect knot in the middle.

I'm starting a second one when I hear a guy's voice.

"Hello? Does this dog have a person?" I follow the voice around to the other side of the hedge, and I see the guy—around my age. He's playing with Rig exactly the way Dad does, pretending to slap the side of Rig's mouth. Rig's doing his chimpanzee imitation. Are all males programmed to play with dogs a certain way?

I always have a hard time talking to new people. It's especially lame being me because my dad is always looking to introduce himself to strangers everyplace he goes. If you could think of a quality in a parent most likely to embarrass a child, I'm pretty sure this is it. Walking down a beach—on vacation!—he's all, *Hey, how you doing? Gorgeous day! Love your umbrella. Great boogie board!* I have been known to pray for quicksand.

"Hi," I say now, aware of how unnatural I sound. Rig, as though he's been busted *(Oh no! Marley caught me playing with a stranger!)*, drops into a perfect obedience school sit.

"Oh, hey," the guy says. When he looks up I can see below his baseball cap that he has smart eyes, a strange light blue. "I'm Jack. I live here." He motions with his chin to the small brown house diagonally across from my dad's. The corners of the two backyards touch. "This dog's yours?"

"Yeah. This is Rig. Well, his real name is Gehrig."

"Gehrig like Lou Gehrig?"

"Exactly," I say.

He looks at my Yankees shirt and grins, which makes his eyes nearly disappear into little slits. He has a long, narrow dimple, like an innie belly button, in his left cheek. "You a Yankees fan?"

"Sure am." I can't believe I said that out loud. I know a lot about the Yankees, but I am quite sure I cannot honestly call myself a fan. I can't figure out a way to unsay it. "I'm Marley," I say. At least that's true.

"Ha—like that dog movie?"

How original. "No, like Marley Baird."

"Your dad's Mr. Baird?"

"Mr. Baird? Robert Baird, yeah. I'm staying with him."

"He teaches at my school."

"You go to Little Valley?"

"Yup. How 'bout you?"

"I'm at Hills East."

"Cool," Jack says.

I nod.

He nods back, eyebrows up.

I nod again.

"This," Jack says, saving us from another round of nodding, "is one great dog." Rig is sitting right in front of Jack, gazing up into his face, like they've known each other forever. Jack rubs each of Rig's ears and then reaches down and picks up a long black vinyl bag. "First day of baseball camp," he says, pointing with his chin, possibly in the general direction of the park. "I'm going early." He seems embarrassed. "You here for the day?"

"No, the whole summer."

"Cool. You just hanging out?"

"No, I'm working. Babysitting some little kid."

"Well," Jack says, lifting his bag up onto his shoulder. "Have fun." He sets off down the street, his bag swinging and hitting him on the shins with every other step, the sound the same as Rig's happy sound: *thump thump thump.*

* * *

When Dad comes into the kitchen, he finds orange juice already poured into the cups and a fresh dandelion bundle on a napkin on his plate. It's a gesture. As Mom would say, I'm making an effort.

Dad glances at the arrangement on his plate and shakes his head, a smile on his face.

"It does look pretty," he says, surprised.

"How come you have so many? Your lawn is, like, covered."

"I wouldn't say it's covered. The landlord lowered the rent because I'm going to tend to the lawn myself. It's just that I wasn't here in April."

"April?" In April he was still in his old new place.

"Dandelion season. I figured a dandelion lover such as yourself would know that."

"So if April is dandelion season, why is your lawn covered with dandelions in July?"

"It's *not* covered, but it's because I wasn't here to get rid of them when they started. If you don't catch the problem when it starts, you're out of luck. Once they turn to seed, that seed spreads all over the yard, and, well, you know how it goes. I will get to it, but in case you haven't noticed, you are looking at a new me, Marley. A more relaxed me. I will get to the weeds when I have the time to do so properly." He examines his bundle. "You didn't pull it out at the root?"

Some *new him*, uptight about the roots. I shrug. "Not really. I wasn't weeding, just picking flowers."

"They're not flowers, Marley. They're weeds."

"To you," I say. "Mom didn't call last night?"

"Hmm?" He's inspecting a fleck of something on the jelly jar lid. "Oh, yes. You were sleeping."

"You should have gotten me up. I really wanted to talk to her."

He scratches at it with his nail until it comes off. "I thought you were exhausted, so I let you sleep." He places the fleck in the center of his napkin, then folds the napkin in quarters.

Yeah, new him. Right.

It's good that he's trying to change, I guess, but couldn't he have tried to new-him himself a year ago? A few years ago? First he had to walk away from our Perfectly Good Life and leave me in this awful two-homes, half-Marley-here/half-Marley-there limbo?

We eat quietly and quickly. Dad brings his plate and cup to the dishwasher and loads them. From the hall he says, "We have to be out of here in ten minutes. You'll be ready?" I hear him close the bathroom door.

When I was really little, Mom liked to sleep late on weekend mornings, and my dad would make a big deal about it. He'd remind me to stay quiet, make it feel like it was something big and wonderful we were doing for my mom. He'd bring me in the bathroom while he shaved. I watched him closely. He rinsed out the sink—thoroughly—every few seconds. One day, he put a pile of shaving cream on the counter next to the sink. "Play," he said. The whole time he shaved, I got to finger-paint with this big mound of shaving cream. It became a weekend tradition. Even then, I totally understood that this was wildly unlike him, that he was always neat, neat, neat and that one does not play with soaps or shaving creams. It was our little weekend secret, a different side of Dad that was all mine.

* * *

He pulls his truck into what must be the Krolls' driveway. There are two bikes with training wheels, a red one piled on a pink one, in front of closed garage doors. The house is white with black shutters. Two shutters are missing.

I climb out and close the door, and at the sound, I hear the bark of a big dog. Dad says I can't bring Rig. He says I need to just concentrate on getting to know the Krolls, finding out how I can be most helpful. So, okay. One day. I can do anything for one day. I survived fishing, right? Mom will find a way to fix this later.

The screen door in front of the house opens and a woman steps out holding a baby. She's not cradling the baby in her arms. The baby's back is against the woman's stomach and chest, and it seems like the woman's hands are pushing hard against its belly. I didn't picture a baby.

A baby! A tiny, totally breakable baby. I don't know how to change diapers. Or how to know when a baby's hungry. I don't even know how to hold a baby—I'd definitely be holding that kid the exact opposite way from how the mom is.

"Robert," the baby's mother says to my dad in a friendly voice. "And you must be Marley."

Her face is so kind. She smiles at me, and there it is again! I have to fight tears. What kind of person gets weepy at a stranger's smile?

I look down at my feet and urge them to walk up the steps. Deep breath. "Hi, Mrs. Kroll."

"Please call me Lynne. So, what has your father told you about us?" she asks, half laughing.

I feel the vibrations of my dad *kalump*ing up the stairs behind me. "Not much, Lynne," he says. "Just that she's here to help you."

"Let's have a seat, while it's still quiet. The girls are watching TV."

Girls! Plural? *S?* And a baby? I turn and glare at my dad, but he's looking straight ahead.

My dad sits on my right; Lynne is on my left. I feel like I'm in the principal's office, even though my father is the one who did something wrong.

"I'm hoping this will be fun for you, Marley. My girls are five, twins. They can be a handful, but they're good girls. I was hoping that you could come over each day, Monday to Friday, and play with them. Just have fun, while I attend to the baby and try to get some work done. I run a business out of the house, and between the baby and the work, and ever since . . . Well, the girls haven't had—"

The door opens and out come two girls in matching pajamas. Matching in that one is wearing Cinderella bottoms with a Snow White top and the other a Cinderella top with Snow White bottoms. They both have long brown hair snaggled in tangles down their backs, and they have the same small brown eyes, too close together. A voice deep inside me is howling, *RUN AWAY, Marley! Run very fast, and do not look back!*

"Who's this?" Cinderella Top asks.

"What are they doing here, Ma?" asks Cinderella Bottoms.

"This is Marley Baird."

I smile and wave a little, looking at one and then the other.

"Marley Bear!"

"Baird," I say.

"Marley Bear!"

"B-A-I-R-D. Baird." But, of course, they're five.

"She's going to come over and play with you two this summer."

"She's big. Why do we have to play with someone that's big? Why can't Jamie just come over?"

"Marley's going to play and help me a little, too. She is in charge."

I'm feeling a little half Cinderella myself: first-half Cinderella. No ball, no coach. Just pathetic servant-girl Cinderella. "What are your names?" I ask them. I'm relieved that Cinderella Top has bangs and Cinderella Bottoms doesn't; otherwise I'm not sure I'd be able to tell them apart, and they'd be able to play tricks on me that probably wouldn't be all that funny.

"I'm sorry, Marley. I forgot. This is Grace," Lynne says, pointing to the girl with bangs. "And this is Faith."

"All right, ladies," my dad says, standing. For the second time in a week, I'm tempted to wrap my arms around a parent's legs and start begging: *Don't leave me!* Then again, I don't even really want to look at him. He wasn't exactly honest with me. Since when does my dad lie?

"I'll pick you up at two, Marley. Maybe we'll play tennis if it cools down a bit." He walks back to his truck.

The girls are staring at me. I force myself to smile, and then think about how forced that smile must look. "Okay," I say. "What do you like to do?"

"Paint," one says. Bangs! Which one has bangs?

"Ride bikes," the other says.

"Does this happen all the time?" I ask Lynne. She looks at me, but it's obvious she didn't hear anything. Or wasn't listening.

"Why don't you play with the girls outside for a while, Marley, and then bring them in for a snack in an hour or so. You'll find a swing set in the back. If they ride their bikes, make sure they wear their helmets."

She takes the baby and walks inside. What kind of mother is that? *Hello?* Just because I was once a kid doesn't mean I know how to do this. Is it legal to leave your kids with someone as ill prepared as I am? Shouldn't I be licensed for this kind of work? Or trained? Will we all be thrown in jail for complete disregard of good old-fashioned common sense? And just by the way, lady, how much will you be paying me?

What if they skin their knees? What if one climbs a tree and gets stuck? What if wasps sting them? Am I supposed to get Lynne or handle it myself? What if I need to pee and there's no one to watch them? Has no one except me taken the time to think this through?

Deep breath. I am way more than twice their age. Okay. I will act like I know what I'm doing. I can trick them into believing I know what I'm doing. Can't I? "Let me see your swing set," I say, and the girls take off around the house. It occurs to me that they're in pajamas and should probably be wearing clothes by now. But Lynne did say to keep them outside.

By the time I reach the backyard, Cinderella Bottoms is swinging by her legs on a trapeze bar, her Snow White top hanging down and covering her face. Cinderella Top is throwing cups full of sand out of an old-looking sandbox and into a bush.

"Nice sandbox," I say. "Wow, you're good at hanging upside down. Do you ever get hurt doing that?"

"Just two times. Wanna see me flip off?"

"Let's just get you down in some nice, normal way." I hold the bar still while she reaches up with her hands and flips her legs down to the ground.

Excellent! I have survived one minute. Two-hundred and ninety-nine more minutes to go.

"What are we gonna do now?" Cinderella Top asks from the sandbox.

"I could push you on the swings."

They snort. At exactly the same time. I'm taking care of mismatched, snorting twins.

"We don't do swings in mornings."

"I'm bored," Cinderella Bottoms says. "Playing with you is boring. I wish Jamie could come over."

Oh, honey, me too.

"Isn't there something *fun* we could do?" Cinderella Top asks.

"Do you want to ride your bikes?"

"I'm ready to do a two-wheeler," Bottoms says. "Mom won't let me until Grace gets ready too. She's always tipping over on her training wheels. And crying. Like a big crying baby that cries a lot."

Cinderella Top—Grace!—looks like she's going to burst into tears. "I have an idea!" I say. Though I don't. I look around. "Do you want to have races?"

"No. Faith always wins. She sort of cheats."

I'm wondering how someone can cheat at a race, though I'm not altogether sure I want to get into it. "Do you want to play tag?"

"It's only good with a lot of people."

I hate this job. I hate my father.

What do kids do? "Hide-and-seek?"

"Need more people," they say at the same time, like I am the dumbest, most clueless *old* person they have ever met.

"Want to sit and look at each other?" They do not

look amused. "What do you do with your mom every day?"

"I don't know."

"Nothing."

"Do you want to pick flowers and surprise your mom with them?"

"We don't have picking flowers," Bottoms— Faith!—says.

"You can always find picking flowers. Come on."

We walk around the yard together, with the twins running off ahead and to the sides, scouring the backyard for flowers.

"I told you so," Faith says, as if she had been expecting a big arrangement of daisies to appear.

I pick through the grass and find some small white clover flowers. We pull those out along with yellow dandelions and tiny buttercups, all of which are mixed in with the grass of their lawn. (It would drive my dad nuts.) I see a forgotten-looking patch of lilies at the back of the yard, half hidden behind some bushes. I tear a few blossoms from the plant.

"Let's find a thing to put them in," Faith says.

"I don't think your mom wanted us inside yet," I say.

"She don't care," says Grace. "Come on."

"No, wait. I know," I say, though again, I don't. What I need is a satchel, filled with enchanting surprises. Including at least one vase. How could I have forgotten my Mary Poppins bag?

Finally I spot the cup that Grace had been using to empty the sandbox. A good makeshift vase. "Is there a hose out here?" I ask. The twins smile in a way that is far more wicked stepsisters than Cinderella and Snow White. They run to the side of the house, push through some bushes, and before I can say, "Change of plan! I'm going home!" I'm soaked. Soaked through. My brain takes a second to register this, since it is a clear blue, not-a-raincloud-in-the-sky, sunshiny morning. My hair is undeniably dripping. They somehow missed most of my shirt, but my shoes are waterlogged. First one little twin head and then another peeks out from behind the bush. "Oops," they say, at the same time.

They don't look one bit sorry. I feel like opening the gate, walking by myself out to the sidewalk, and finding my way home. It's not like they could take my license away. I have no license for this!

I am so mad, I forget which one is which. "You," I say, pointing at Cinderella Bottoms. "Go inside and get me a towel. And you," I say, pointing at Cinderella Top.

"You." But I can't think of anything. I need a manual! Where's the manual?

Cinderella Bottoms looks at her sister, and then me. She smirks and starts slowly toward the house.

"Faster," I say. Bottoms runs a few steps before settling back into a slow-paced walk.

"You," I say again, "have angered a Marley Bear."

"So what?"

"So, you do not want to anger the Marley Bear."

"Why not?" Cinderella Top asks.

Why not. "Because the Marley Bear is in charge?"

I'm flailing. I'm sinking. I'm drowning in wet sneakers.

Cinderella Bottoms is running toward us. Faith! Bottoms is Faith! She hands me a torn gray towel. I feel them both watching me as I rub it through my hair, wipe off my shoes. I turn my back to them and slip out of my shoes and place them on a rusting metal table to dry. Then I turn with a growl, my arms over my head, hands curved into claws. "Angry! Marley! Bear!" I say.

The twins shriek with pleasure (I think), and head back to the swing set. I chase them around, beating up my bare feet, until I run out of breath. While I'm leaning against the splintery side bars of the swing set, I spot some chalk poking out of the sandbox.

Chalk. I can do something with chalk. I pick it up and the Dad's-classroom smell of it makes me mad all over again at my stupid father for getting me into this stupid babysitting situation. I lead the girls to their driveway, where I draw a hopscotch outline. We find pebbles and play a competitive match of hopscotch.

Faith is not what I'd call a gracious winner. Her victory dance involves a lot of butt shaking and taunting in her sister's face. As Grace's eyes well up, I suggest we go inside for a snack.

The inside of the Krolls' house is a mess. There are papers everywhere, pairs of shoes and single shoes scattered against the wall in the hallway and under the table in the kitchen. The sink and counter next to it are piled high with dirty dishes and cereal bowls. There's a milk container, beaded with little water drops, just sitting on the counter. I hear Lynne talking fast—she must be on the phone.

"Kwee have gummy bears?" Faith asks.

"No. No candy in the morning." I'm making this up, but it sounds right.

"Kwee have chocolate milk?"

How should I know? There must be rules. I know *I* couldn't have chocolate milk in the morning, but what do I know about what these two can and cannot do? "How about some bananas?" I ask, after spotting some borderline brown ones on the counter.

"Banana taffy?" Faith asks.

"No. Just bananas. Plain."

"Uh, no?" Grace says.

If I think about the number of hours I have left today before I get to go home—no, not even home. Dad's place. Ouch.

I hear steps approaching and then Lynne is in the kitchen, putting the phone back on the wall. "Marley, you're wet," she says. I am. I am wet. And my feet keep sticking to the tile floor, as if I'm walking through the remains of an old syrup spill.

Lynne pulls some bowls out of the refrigerator and puts them in front of the twins. It might be their leftover breakfast, and it doesn't look too inviting, but at least they're sitting, fairly quiet, and eating. I think of that scene in *The Sound of Music* when Maria, the children's new governess, is speaking to the children's father at the dinner table, and listing the mean-spirited things the children had done to her. She disguises the children's bad intentions as friendly and welcoming until all the children at the table are crying from guilt over how they treated poor Maria. I wish I had an acoustic guitar waiting on the front porch so I could lead Top and Bottoms in a rousing round of "My Favorite Things."

But one thing has already become very, very clear: these children are no Von Trapps.

* * *

After they finish their snack, I help the twins get dressed. I have to admit, it's sort of fun to look at their little clothes and dress them up. I was never into dolls, but putting clothes on little humans is more fun than you might think.

We play in their room. I help them make a city out of blocks and suggest they let their stuffed animals be the rulers and the dolls their servants. They love making the stuffed animals boss the dolls around.

I make peanut butter and jelly sandwiches for lunch, with the crusts cut off. After lunch, we sit on the hill by their house and watch wild rabbits.

"Did you see that one, the way its white tail bopped when it was hopping?" I ask them.

They nod. "There's always rabbits here," Faith tells me. "They live here."

The bunnies sit, completely still, then race across the hill. They don't seem to have a moment of acceleration at all—they go from still to speeding almost at once, with a run, run, hop motion. There's something hypnotic about the bunnies, and I enjoy their effect on the twins. It's the first time all day the girls haven't been in some kind of frantic motion. Even when they sit and eat at the table, they're usually tapping a foot or wobbling a cup back and forth.

"My father always kept bunnies away from our house," I tell them. "He'd catch them in traps and set them free in a park."

"Your daddy hates bunnies?" Grace asks.

"He's a real garden kind of guy. He doesn't like how bunnies eat all the bulbs before tulips and other flowers have a chance to grow. The wild rabbits used to eat all the vegetables in his garden before he had a chance to pick them."

"That's bad," Grace says.

"I guess," I say. "I'd happily give up fresh broccoli to watch a bunny go bounding up this hill."

"I'd give up fresh broccoli for . . . um . . . for no broccoli," Grace says.

"How come we're just sitting?" Faith asks. "Don't you have to play with us?"

"Sometimes it's nice to just sit, isn't it?"

"Not for me. Mommy said you have to play with us. You should have to do what we want."

"Not exactly," I say. "I'm pretty sure she said you have to listen to me."

"I'm gonna tell," Faith says.

Please do, I think. *Tell your mother this is not working out. PLEASE.*

I just look at her. She glares right back into my eyes.

"Faith," Grace says. "You're making Marley Bear mad."

"I don't care."

You and me both, Faith.

"Look, Faith. I'm a bunny!" Grace hops over the flat bottom of the hill. She stops, totally still. She pretends to eat a carrot, *chomp chomp,* and then hops again. Faith hops behind Grace, steps up her hopping to catch up with Grace, then knocks her down so she can hop over her. I think I have some kind of idea what Grace meant when she said that Faith cheats at races. The twins chase each other around the house a few dozen times.

When I hear Dad's truck pull up, I take the twins from the backyard into the den. I walk into the back room, where Lynne is sitting at a computer, bouncing the baby's seat with the toes of her right foot. The baby's big head looks heavy, rolling from side to side, ready for sleep. "What's up, Marley?" She keeps typing as she talks, her eyes on the screen.

"My dad's here."

"Already? I feel like I just sat down and got the baby—" She looks up at the clock and then at me. She smiles, like she's holding in a laugh. "Are you okay?"

I know that my hair looks funny when it dries by itself. I look down and see mud streaks over my new Yankees shirt. I look as though I've been tortured. "I think I feel the same way I look," I say. Then I gasp, because that's the kind of thing you should think but probably not say to the mother of the torturing party. I can see my babysitting report card: Needs work on social skills.

Lynne just smiles again. "It'll get easier." She looks at her computer screen, then quickly back at me. I'm standing there, waiting for cash. Does she think I'm doing this for free? She just looks at me until the room's about to explode from awkward. "If it's okay with you, I'll pay you on Fridays," she finally says.

Oh no you won't. I'm not coming back. But I can't bring myself to say that. "Okay," I say.

* * *

I'm free! I can watch TV or read a book or stare into the distance for a few minutes without a crazy five-year-old climbing a tree or threatening to jump off the top of a swing set onto my head. I climb into the truck like a lost person saved from utter exhaustion and complete dehydration by a passerby. I slide down in the seat. Then I remember that this passerby is the reason I feel as burned out as I do.

"Wow," my dad says. "I'm guessing you don't want to play tennis now?"

"Can't move."

"They wore you out?"

"Totally and completely. I don't want to go back, Dad."

"It'll get easier," he says.

"No. I mean it. I really, really don't want to go back." The words are just tumbling out, and as always these days, the tears are threatening. "Like, I can't go back."

"I've had a long day, too," Dad says.

Why can't he just listen? And agree with me for once? "This is . . . Ugh, just forget it."

"What?"

"This is . . . You didn't tell me there'd be twins. You made it sound like there was just one kid."

"People say it's easier when there's more than one kid, because they play with each other."

"People don't know what they're talking about." My head is throbbing. Maybe because my teeth are clenched so tight.

"It'll get easier, Marley. It really will."

He doesn't have a clue.

Just Outside the World of Real Rabbits

W hen we pull up to his place, the sun is tucked behind heavy clouds. There's a small, easy-to-miss patch of grass that is totally dandelion-free—the spot where I picked this morning—but the rest of the lawn is freckled with dandelions low to the ground. This morning, they'd been all perky. Now they look worn out from a day of reaching toward the sun.

I let Dad unlock the door and I walk in ahead of him. Rig comes running over to me, his tail wagging so hard, it's practically going in circles. "Hey, hey," I say. I kneel down to hug him and he licks my cheek hard and looks at my face for a second before he licks it hard again. Those hard licks are something like the kind of hug you give someone when you've missed them—tighter, like you're trying to squeeze the love into them. I hug him again and stand up. Then he turns his attention to Dad.

I take my phone into my room.

Leah doesn't answer her cell. Jane's cell is off. Ugh, house phones. Jane's mother says she'll tell Jane to call me back as soon as she gets home.

I need my friends!

I try Mom but get her voice mail. My parents are both kind of like the Amish or something when it comes to cell phones. Mom's not even that old, but for some reason, she always panics when her cell phone rings—as if someone would only call it if there were a true emergency. She's decades ahead of my dad, though. He refuses to even get a cell. And they hardly ever call mine—it's kind of a miracle that I even have one. They only call the house phone. Who does that? Obvious answer: only my parents and, possibly, the Amish.

I'm going crazy here.

I lie on my bed, wondering what I'd do if I were at

Mom's. Duh. "Hey, Dad! Where's your computer?"

"Broken."

"When will it be fixed?"

"As soon as I have some money to pay for it."

Can it get any worse?

"Couldn't you have told me so I could bring mine? How am I supposed to check e-mail and—"

"Thank you for your concern about my broken computer," he says. "If you get desperate, they have computers at the library."

I'd better get to the library. I'll need some books to help pass this time—all this time.

Talk about an endless summer.

"Marley, could you come out here, please?"

"Whaaaat?" I yell from the bed.

"I need some help."

I stomp out of bed and into the living room. "What?"

He points at some boxes stacked neatly along the living room wall. "I got through most of my boxes the first three days, but I haven't done anything since. I'm scared that if I don't do this now, they'll still be here when you and your children come visit me in a few hundred years."

"My children and I will have other plans," I say.

"Very nice, Marley. Come on. Be a pal. I need to get this done."

"That sounds like a lot of fun," I say, my voice flat. If he didn't want to unpack boxes, then maybe he shouldn't have moved out.

"Why are you being like this?"

"Do you really not know?"

I'd like to tell him how furious I am. How I hate the stupid job he's making me do and acting like I can't quit even though all he'd have to do is say, "Sorry. It's not working out because you have two wild banshee twins and my daughter never agreed to it anyway."

I know it sounds crazy, but I have no idea how to talk to him. Once he makes up his mind about something, that's it. When I was in third grade, he said I couldn't eat peanut butter and Fluff sandwiches anymore because Fluff was junk. When I showed him that jelly, which I was allowed to eat, wasn't any better for me, he wouldn't change his ruling. His reason? "Fluff is unnaturally white." Unnaturally white! That's not the kind of guy you can reason with.

"I just need some time," I say. "To myself. I don't want to unpack boxes. I'd rather sit and stare at the wall until my friends come over."

He goes through all his gestures of disgust, just like I knew he would. First the whole creepy lip-lifting action that used to make my mother laugh behind her hand. Then the air cough. Finally, he shuts his eyes and shakes his head quickly. "You couldn't say that nicely? You couldn't just say, 'I'd like to relax for a little while if that's okay'?"

"I want to be alone," I say.

"As well you should be. First take these boxes of trash to the garage with me. Oh, and this one"—he points at a neater box by itself on the other wall—"is something your mother left for when you were in a grumpy mood and needed something to do. I'd say now seems like a good time to mention it."

He lifts up a few of his boxes, and points with his foot at one he wants to have. I peek inside and see my Monopoly game, the very one Jane and Leah and I have been using forever. The one with money still warped out of shape from being drenched in the first Water Balloon Blitz.

"Hey! Don't throw out my Monopoly," I say as I follow him.

"I got you a new one." He puts the boxes down against the garage wall, next to some others, and stretches his arms up over his head. "I looked inside and there were only three pieces left: the hat, the dog, and, uh—"

"The shoe," I say. Jane is always the shoe. Leah is the hat.

"I thought you'd enjoy a new one."

"Oh. Well, thank you." I see it for what it is—a Robert Baird Gesture. I leave the carton with the old Monopoly game in the garage, then go right in my room and close the door.

The truth is, it's not my room. Not at all. It's boring and foreign and I want to go home. I'm sorry, but it's not in any way normal for one person, one teenage person, to be expected to live in two different homes. Joint custody is a monumentally bad idea.

When I started staying overnight at Dad's first new place, his old new place, by the time I got used to being with him it was time to go to school or home. I was always getting used to being with one parent when I was sent back to the other one. At least at his old new place, I'd known it was temporary. He had rented a small apartment at this complex where a lot of divorced dads live. I knew just from looking at it that he wouldn't be able to stay there. The lawn was pure brown, just dead, as though no one even bothered trying to water it. It was an until-I-find-someplace-else place. Or, as I liked to think, an until-we-work-things-out-and-I-move-back-home place.

And what's up with Mom? Maybe her Facebook friends have taught her how to use her cell phone. I text her:

Mom. Impt. Call. Need 2 talk 2 U.

Oh! That box!

I go back to the living room and take the box Mom left for me back to the room that's my room only doesn't feel like my room.

Mmm. Books. My mom left me a box of books! The one on top is the latest in my favorite series—I had no idea that was even out! God, I love my mom.

I'm about to start reading when I see a plastic something sticking up in the corner. A bag of balloons. No, bags. Lots of bags of balloons.

Hmm.

I think about when I can get Leah and Jane—a huge surprise attack. Coming out of Curtain Call? A trap at the park? Setting them up to walk under that little bridge near the elementary school? Oh, this is fun! I've actually invented summer fun in the absence of actual summer fun.

I read and then I do what I told my dad I was going

to do. I stare at the wall until I fall asleep. I must sleep through dinner, because when I wake up, a strange pre-dawn light is touching the corners of the window.

This morning, I know where I am—there's Rig and the light blue walls. I'm at Dad's. Wow. I must have been really exhausted to sleep so long. There's something nagging, tugging at me. Oh, man. Twins. And Mom didn't call. I have to spend another whole day with in-sane five-year-olds. I close my eyes and fall back into that not-awake/not-asleep place until Rig lets out one of his pitiful whimpers. He needs to pee. Badly.

It's a beautiful Crayola-sky morning. The air doesn't have the tiniest bit of cool to it, and if it's this warm this early, it's going to be a long, hot day with Tweedledee and Tweedledum. Rig trots off toward the bushes, and I sit down in another patch of dandelions. I have an idea for keeping the twins busy, and I gather a bunch of dandelions together to bring to their house. I seek out the ones with the longest stems and throw them into one of Dad's empty plastic planters.

"Ruh." Rig's greeting.

"Marley, you there?"

Jack! Why does he talk so loud in the morning? I walk around the bush and Rig does it again. He gets that guilty *Busted!* look *(Oh, man! Marley caught me talking to the fun boy!)* and drops his behind right into a proper sit.

"Hey, Jack. How's it going?"

"It's going."

"How was camp?"

He seems to literally cringe at the word *camp*. "It was good. So how was that kid?"

"Kids!" I say. Rig walks his front paws out in front of him until he's lying down. He looks at Jack, then rolls onto his back. Without a pause, Jack starts scratching Rig's belly. "Twin girls," I say, "with a freaky amount of energy."

"You have to watch two kids? That's like twice as, uh—"

"Actually, there are three, but the baby just stays with the mom." Rig's rear paw pounds out its happy noise against the ground: *thump, thump, thump*.

"You're going back today?"

I nod.

He looks down at his dirty black cleats, then asks, "You around this weekend?"

"Oh, yeah," I make myself say. "All weekend." I wonder why he's asking. I also wonder why this guy

with intense light blue eyes is hanging around talking to *me*.

"Um, Marley? What's your dog doing?"

Rig is up and on the prowl. He freezes, ears back,
his front paws down and his butt high up in the air, then
chases something invisible, stops, and tries to bite it. I
walk closer and hear the *zzzz* of a fly. Rig runs a few
steps and snaps at the air again. Then he runs around a
tree and puts his feet up on it, as though he could climb
it. He sits, looks patiently around, then lies down in de-
feat. If you didn't know he was chasing a fly, you'd have
to assume that he was going through some kind of ca-
nine psychotic break, or performing an interpretive
dance.

"He's never caught a fly," I say. "It's his major goal
in life."

Jack looks at his watch.

"Well, I'll see ya." Jack bends down to rub Rig's
ears, then picks up his bag. I watch him until he rounds
the corner toward the park.

* * *

I call Mom's cell phone again before and after breakfast and get her voice mail. I call Leah early too.

"Marley! I was going to call you!"

I have the phone between my shoulder and ear, and it keeps sliding as I make my bed. "I wish you had!" I say. Why isn't anyone calling me?!

"I know. I feel awful. OH! My God. You have no idea. I didn't know what this was going to be like!"

"What what was going to be like?"

"Curtain Call. It's just intense. There is no other way to describe it. It is *so* intense. The people, they're, like, amazing, so it's great. Jane and I are the youngest ones in the upper division, and there are all these people from Roosevelt High and—"

"You guys have to come over today."

"I'm not sure we—"

"I'm desperate. Please." I lower my voice, but not a lot. "I'm going to kill my father. I'm babysitting for psycho twins, and I need you guys. I just do."

"Trust me, Marley. I want to. It's just that we have all this work we need to get done, and—"

"Leah. I never beg you. Please. Come over this afternoon. Please!"

"I'll talk to Jane," she says. "We'll try."

* * *

At the twins' house, I start the day with an advantage over yesterday: no surprise element. I know what I'm getting: two. This time, before they can start jumping off swing sets or turning a hose on me, I show them my big container of dandelions.

"Is that weeds?" Grace asks.

I sit down at the rusty old metal table and pull out the dandelions one by one. "You think these are weeds?"

They nod their heads, then look at each other, then nod their heads again. I have a feeling they watch a lot of TV.

"I see jewelry."

"You're a weird bear," Grace says.

"And you're a funny girl," I say. That makes her smile, then look at Faith to see if she's catching the smile.

"Did you ever make a daisy chain?" I ask them. They shake their heads. "We're going to make bracelets out of these jewels."

"I don't like jue-ry," Faith says.

"Oh, so then you wouldn't want a fairy crown either?"

"Oh, I like crowns," Faith says.

"I want one!" Grace says.

"I'll make two, if you guys can help. Go around and gather up all the dandelions you can find. Look for ones like this," I say, picking one up, "with long stems. They make the best chains."

"I'm gonna find more than you," Faith says.

"Nuh-uh," Grace says. "I'm a better looker. Mommy always says."

Their little twin-whine voices bicker as they set off to different corners of the yard. I get two tiaras going, enjoying the relative quiet. I don't think I'm cut out for babysitting, but I know my way around a dandelion.

Using my thumb, I split the stalk just about half an inch, up close near the flower. I thread the stem of the next one through and do the same to its stalk. By the time the girls show up with their last piles of dandelions, my hands are covered in the sticky, milky fluid that leaks out of the stems. Two crowns are almost done. I push the yellow head of a dandelion through the stem and try it on Faith's head. It's a little too big, so I take out one flower and try again. Perfect. I do the same for Grace.

"What do fairy princesses do?" Grace asks.

"Well, they treat each other very nicely," I say. "And they are always very kind to their babysitters."

Faith looks disgusted. "That's so stupid."

"And boring," Grace says.

"And stupid."

"Let's be nasty fairy princesses," Grace says.

"Yeah, the nastiest!" Faith says, and they're off again, nasty-fairy-princessing each other all over the yard. There's something about those crowns that takes the edge off—a tiny bit of magic that makes them a bit more bearable. Each time one runs over to me, about to whine about the way Grace poked her or Faith said something that hurt her feelings, I sprinkle fairy dust on her (tiny bits of yellow dandelion petals that fell on the table). Sometimes, they just run away, twirling like fairies, mostly smiling, and dancing around the yard.

* * *

"Marley Bear?" Grace says at lunch.

"Yes?"

"Could you catch us a bunny later?"

"Why would you want to catch a bunny?"

"To have it," Faith says. "Duh, Marley."

"Don't 'duh' me. You don't want to anger the Marley Bear."

"That's true," Faith says.

"So could you?" Grace asks.

"I don't think I could," I say, turning to the sink to start washing the dishes that have been there since breakfast (though I'm not sure which day's breakfast). I wonder what my father would think of the chaos that is the Kroll house. I bet even the new-him dad would be disgusted. "Those bunnies live outside. They don't belong to people."

"It could," Faith says. "If you caught one. It could be our pet."

I turn the water off, wondering if Lynne would even want me washing her dishes. Maybe she'd be embarrassed, annoyed that I decided her dishes shouldn't be crookedly stacked on the counter, crusted with food. Where's the manual? I'm never sure what the right thing to do is.

"The bunnies do too belong to us. They're on our hill!" Grace says.

I turn the water back on. It has to be better to have someone help you, right? I rinse the dishes under the tap.

"I don't think the rabbit would be happy." I carefully place the clean plates on top of the already overflowing drying rack.

"I'd be happy," Grace says.

"Me too," Faith says. "And the rabbit would too. It would like us."

"I just like watching them," I say. "If you stuck one in a cage, it wouldn't be right. Those bunnies have been free to go wherever they want since they could hop. How would you feel if someone stuck you in a little and told you you couldn't leave?"

"I'm not a bunny!" Faith yells.

"No, you're not. I can tell because bunnies don't wear Little Mermaid shirts."

Faith laughs. "And my ears are smaller."

"But not a lot."

Faith makes a face and starts to touch her ears.

"Are you guys done?"

"I'm still drinking my milk," Grace says.

"Want to bring it outside?"

"Mom doesn't let us," Faith says.

"I think it'll be okay."

"Then *I'm* taking *mine, too.*" Her taunty voice climbs my spine.

I put their plates in the sink, and then we head out for our quiet after-lunch bunny-watching time.

When you look from a distance, it can take a while to spot a bunny. First all you can see are their twitchy little ears. Then you find the face between the ears. Then, as though they feel you staring, they take off, and there's that bobbing tail. Every time I see it, it just thrills me. I must have read too many Beatrix Potter books when I was little.

"Do you guys know all the great bunny stories, like Peter Rabbit?"

Grace spits her milk out in a spray that ends up largely in Faith's hair. Faith yells "HEY!" and knocks over her milk so it spills onto Grace's lap. Grace stands, and I race between them and hold them apart.

"She spit her milk at me!" Faith yells, furious.

I bend over so I can see Grace's face. "Why did you do that?"

There's white liquid all over her. She's trying to find her voice, but she keeps sucking in air.

"Are you choking?"

She shakes her head. She's practically wheezing.

"Are you laughing?" She nods.

I'm scared that I'll soon be witness to the dreaded milk-out-the-nostrils show, but I'm spared. Finally, she says, "A rabbit named Peter? That's so funny." She looks at Faith, then me. Then back at Faith. And back at me. "Isn't it?"

"I think a computer named Peter is funnier," Faith says.

"No," Grace says. "A duck with the name of that boy from school. Felipe. A duck named Felipe."

"A garbage can named Susan."

"A zebra named Tyler," Grace says. "That's the funniest."

"No, I have a funnier one. A dog named Dog. That's funny. Right?"

"No. A tree named Dog. That's the best."

"You know what's funnier? A cat named Dog. THAT is funny."

This might continue for the rest of the day. How did it even start? Right: Peter Rabbit. I remember that long ago, Peter's name was what I liked best. He had siblings with these totally rabbit names: Flopsy, Mopsy, and Cottontail. Then there was Peter. Hello? Whose idea was that? I always assumed that Peter got himself into all that trouble because he felt like he didn't belong, like he was just outside the world of real rabbits, not quite one of the crowd.

When Am I Ever Mad?

∞

My dad tries to get me to play tennis with him after work. I have less than no interest in spending time with the person who put me in this situation. I'm mad at him. And at my absent, doesn't-check-her-messages mother.

Anyway, I'm hoping Leah and Jane will come over. I sit in the living room, looking out the front window to the street, Rig at my side.

I get bored waiting. I find that bag of balloons and fill up a few. A small, just-the-three-of-us blitz could never win back the title, but it would be fun anyway.

I try the kitchen sink. The faucet's spout is too big, so I work in the bathroom. I attach the balloon and remember to fill it slowly. It flies right off anyway and soaks me. Nice.

I try again, with the water even slower. Good. It starts to come back to me. Water balloons that are filled only a little are easier to handle but take more force to break. It's tempting to fill them just to the point of bursting, because those are the best for a blitz—there's an immediate break and soak upon hitting the target. They're hard to handle, though—they sometimes break just from holding them.

I make a big pile. I take the kitchen garbage and throw it in the outside bin and stash the balloons in the kitchen trash basket.

And I sit and wait for them to show.

When I see Jane's mother's car pull into my dad's driveway, I nearly fall to the ground in full-body relief. Thank God!

As soon as I open the door, things are better, tolerable.

But different. What's different?

"Jane! When did you get glasses?"

"Last week," she says, smiling, reaching up to touch them.

I cannot believe how different they make her look. Usually the big moment in the makeover scene happens when the plain girl takes off her glasses and the audience realizes she's beautiful. For Jane, apparently, it's the opposite.

"They look so fantastic."

"She knows," Leah says. "That's why she got them."

"Yeah, it had nothing to do with needing to, I don't know, see?" I say.

Jane shoots Leah a *shut up* look, then says, "Let's just say that sometimes, like when you really want glasses, that giant *E* can be *really* hard to read."

Whatever. I'm so glad they're here!

I give them the tour. "This is the bathroom. This is the other bathroom. This is my room," I say. "My room here."

"Why are your bags on the dresser?" Jane asks. "Can't you put your stuff in drawers?" Her eyes are on the mirror above my dresser.

I slide open the top drawer. It's empty. "I could, yeah. I guess I just didn't have a chance yet."

"Will you leave stuff here and have the stuff that's here and the stuff that's at your mom's?" Leah asks. Without giving me a second to answer, she says, "My cousins? The ones who live in Westport? They have two of everything! Like, they have a wardrobe at their mother's house and one at their father's house. They have video games at both places, computers. All that. It's, like, twice as good."

I lead them out of the room. I point at my father's room. "That's my dad's. Here's the kitchen. Isn't it the most depressing house you've ever seen?"

Jane walks in behind me. "What do you have to eat?" God, she looks great.

"Hang on. I missed something. Can't you hurt your eyes wearing glasses if you don't need them?"

"The prescription's not strong," Jane says. "And even if I don't really need them, I kind of really need them. I love them!"

Okay.

We look in the refrigerator while Leah starts opening cabinet doors. "Where's the junk?" she says. "There's nothing to eat here."

My fingers are kind of itching to reach into the trash and pull out those water balloons and slam them. My father would have an insane fit if I did something like that in his kitchen, and my friends know him well enough to award tons of bonus points for bravery. Or stupidity. I want the title. But I know this doesn't even come close to Leah's blitz. I'd need tons more witnesses. It would be so fun, though!

Once we get ourselves Diet Cokes, we're just sort of looking at each other. "My room?" I ask.

Before long, Leah's on my bed and Jane's sitting on the floor, leaning against the dresser. Just like that, my room here seems brighter, happier.

"You won't believe this, Marley. We have so much to tell you," Jane says.

"What won't she believe? About Sage?"

"No. Shut up, Leah. That was nothing."

"Right. Twenty-five minutes of nothing."

"What are you talking about?" I ask.

Leah leans forward like she has a great story to tell. "There are, like, twenty of us in our division at Curtain Call, okay? There are all these really cool people from Roosevelt. I mean, it's us and all these high school people."

"So who's Sage?" I ask.

"It's nothing," Jane says, glaring a little at Leah.

"Yeah," I say. "It really sounds like nothing. Okay."

"It's just this guy, this sophomore, who got really into it when we had to do these relaxation exercises together. I mean, he was just really into it." She starts laughing, then watches herself in the mirror, laughing.

"Really into *her*," Leah says. "And I like the way you didn't even mention that improv you guys did. Like that never happened." She picks up the fringe of the bedspread and starts to braid it. "Marley, I wish you were doing Curtain Call, too. It's amazing."

"Yeah, it sounds just the tiniest bit better than hanging out with five-year-old freaks."

"It sucks?" Jane asks.

"Totally."

"It's only been two *days*," Leah says with this new, weird bad-actress delivery. "How awful could it *be?*"

"Let's just not even talk about it. Tell me more about this guy," I say to Jane.

"It's no big deal," Jane says.

We always talk about guys, but whatever. "Do you want to just play Monopoly?"

"I guess," Leah says, dramatic enthusiasm gone.

I walk out to the garage to get the old Monopoly game. In the yard I see a ball flying back and forth. I open the door. There's Dad, playing catch with Jack. Yeah, okay. Sure. Dad sees me holding the game and asks, "Why don't you use the new one I got you?"

"Where is it?"

"My closet."

"Okay," I say. Then, because we're just looking at each other, I say, "Hi, Jack." I would like to ask why he is playing catch with my father. It's too weird, though. Words won't form.

"Hey, Marley."

I stash the old Monopoly game back in the garage and head back inside, but not before Leah's next to me, looking.

"Who's the guy?"

"Jack. He lives there," I say, pointing.

"He's kind of hot."

"Who's hot?" Jane asks as we walk into the kitchen.

"It's nothing. It's this neighbor, Jack."

"Do you like him?" Jane asks.

"I don't really know him."

"And what does *that* have to do with anything?" Leah says with this big, weird hand motion, as if she's performing for someone with bad vision in the last row of a huge auditorium.

"I'll get the game," I say.

Dad's new room is so . . . Dad. In his closet, his teacher shirts are all hanging the same distance from each other, like in an ad for some closet organization system. His shoes are still in the boxes they came in, neatly spaced along the floor. Sweaters are stacked in perfectly sized containers on the left. Sitting all by itself on a shelf at the back is the Monopoly game. I start pulling off the plastic wrap as I walk back to the kitchen table.

This new game feels so different. Not a single corner is frayed or ripped. It's all so crisp, like my dad's version of the world—everything in its place. I hadn't realized how used to the feel of the old game I was. That money was so soft and water-warped; the Community Chest and Opportunity Knocks card corners were all rounded.

Jane hands out the money, slapping the crisp bills down into little piles. She's always the banker.

It feels so great to be playing Monopoly with my friends again!

Leah takes the hat, Jane takes the shoe, and I take the dog. We all roll to see who goes first. I get double sixes; a very good sign. I get to go first.

We haven't even made it around the board once yet when the phone rings. "Don't play without me," I say, stepping into the living room.

"Hello?"

"Marley! God, I miss you!"

"Mom! Why didn't you call me?"

"I did call. You were sleeping. And I'm calling you now. Why? Is everything okay?"

"It is so not okay."

"What?"

"Did you know Daddy got me a job?"

"He said he had something lined up, yes."

"Well, did you know he just *told* me about it? He didn't even ask me. I mean, it's awful and I don't want a job and he can't just do that, right?"

She's quiet for a few seconds. "I think this is between the two of you, Marley."

"What?!"

"What does your father say?"

"That I need something to do. That I can't back out because he made a commitment to the twins' mother."

"There are two of them?"

"Exactly."

"Well, I'm sure they keep you busy. Why don't you just talk to your father some more about it?"

"He doesn't listen. You have to talk to him." She has to. That's how it works. "He won't listen," I say again.

"I can't tell him what to do when you're staying with him. You two need to work it out together."

"He's not willing to work it out. It's a whole do-as-I-say thing."

"I'm sorry you don't like your job. I really am. Try to make the best of it. I'll call you when I get to Yumi's.

I'm still at Louise's, for the rest of the week. I'll try to remember to check messages if you need to reach me, okay?"

"Yeah. Thanks a lot."

"I know this is hard. All three of us have a lot to figure out. It's new for all of us. I'm not used to missing my girl. I really miss you. It's hard for me too."

I'm so mad. What exactly are you supposed to do when a problem has no solution?

"Marley, did you get that box?"

"Yeah, thanks for the books," I say.

"And balloons. Did you blitz yet?"

I think of the balloons waiting in the kitchen, how easy it would be to sneak attack them right now.

"Not yet. Isn't there something you can do? I've been waiting for you, to talk to you, to fix this, and—"

"I'm sorry, Marley. I love you."

"You too. Bye."

I feel like throwing something. Something way heavier than a water balloon. Or sweeping all the plates off a set table with my arm, like in a movie, but I just go back to the kitchen and sit down. It's my turn. I get sent to jail. I probably could have predicted that. I do a forward roll on the kitchen floor. (We added that one in third grade, when we were all into gymnastics.) And I move the dog to jail. When Leah takes her turn and lands on St. James, she just buys it and hands the dice to Jane. Jane rolls.

"Hello?" I say.

"What?" Jane says.

"What?" Leah says, annoyed.

"Did you maybe forget something, Leah?"

"I paid!" She looks down. "And I took the card. What?"

"You didn't do your jumping jacks. I mean, duh? St. James? Ten jumping jacks?

"Can't we just skip that part?" Leah says.

Skip it? Why play?

"I'm sorry," Leah says. "We're just tired, Marley. CC is, like, really intense."

When I land on Boardwalk I try to help them get into the game by really hamming it up, singing the whole introduction to "Under the Boardwalk." When it comes time for them to sing backup ("under the boardwalk, boardwalk!"), they're not even halfhearted. They're probably not even quarter-hearted.

"Whoa," I say, stopping midsong. "You call yourselves acting students?"

"To be honest, Marley, I guess I'm not really in the mood for Monopoly," Leah says.

"Really?"

"Thank God," Jane says, "because I cannot play that game another minute."

"So what *do* you want to do?" I ask.

"I have so much to do for tomorrow," Leah says. "We're supposed to practice these exercises for movement class." She starts putting away the board.

"I'll do it," I say.

Leah takes out her phone and I hear her ask her mom to pick them up now. Jane brings the Diet Coke cans to the counter. "We have to meet up with our class partners for scene work later," Jane says. "We really just wanted to come over and see you and hang for a while. We have so much to do."

"Oh, well," I say. "I'm glad you could come." I put the bills and cards, the dog, hat, and shoe back in the box.

"Don't be *mad*, Marley," Leah says as she comes back into the room.

"When am I ever mad?" I say, fitting the snug top back on the Monopoly box. "So whose house for the Fourth this year? Do you guys wanna come here?"

They look at each other. Then Leah says, "Why don't you come to Jane's?"

"Yeah," Jane says. "I might invite some people from CC, but you should definitely come."

"You have to meet them, Marley. They're really great."

"Will Sage be there?" I ask, teasing like a fourth-grade boy.

"You have got to see this guy, Marley," Leah says. "He is so hot and he is so into Jane. I mean, OH! My God!"

"All right," I say. "So you want to get together tomorrow or Thursday or something?"

"We're going to be so busy, but the Fourth is what, Friday? We'll just see you then, okay? Oh, and you won't believe this, but I got my parents to agree to stay inside the whole time!"

"At a pool party?" Her mom is so neurotic—there's no way.

"I know! I talked them into a lifeguard."

"WHAT?"

"I know! Do you know Joe Perkovich? The really tall one? On the basketball team?"

I don't. But wow. A high school lifeguard and no parents.

*　*　*

[83]

My brain is scanning ahead. I know one thing. Forget that stupid amateur stash in the kitchen trash. I will blitz Leah and Jane at this party. It's kind of brilliant, but maybe a little too obvious. No, mostly brilliant. It meets all the requirements: School's over. Not a ton of days have passed since the last day of school, unless I make the case that this counts as the number of days that have passed since the last day of school *last* year, since no one has blitzed anyone else since then. Plus bonus points for courage! It's at a party! People I don't know will be there. That totally takes courage!

I will win back the blitzing crown on the Fourth.

Unless one of them gets me first.

Slightly Painful Beginnings

W hen my dad picks me up from the Krolls' on Wednesday, he has our tennis rackets in the back of the truck.

"I'm too wiped," I say. "Faith stuck gum in Grace's hair. Twice. They wouldn't eat the lunch I made them, and—"

"Then just a quick volley," he says.

He drives to the park by Mom's house, and I feel this wave of longing as we drive by.

"It's been too long since we played," he says. "Let's have some fun."

I may have figured something out. It seems very possible that my dad does not know the correct definition of *fun*.

I'm not very good at tennis, even though both my parents are. Sometimes, and I never know when it'll be, I play really well. It's so weird, because the next time I'll be whacking the ball over the fence or just barely getting it over the net, but every now and then, it all comes together.

Dad and I play for almost an hour. There are balls everywhere (this not being one of the days I play well). Even though I didn't want to play, I'm getting some pleasure out of whacking the ball. It's not exactly a five-year-old's head I'm picturing, but it's not that far off, either.

"Let's gather up the balls and hit one more round," Dad says. He walks around the inside perimeter of the fence, and I step out through the gate to hunt down the balls I hit out.

It's right there for me to see. Still, it takes a minute to get it. First I see the bizarre pink and yellow of Leah's sister's old hand-me-down bike. I think, *Wow, I have to tell Leah there's someone else riding around with that same awful bike.* Then I notice another girl walking in a big group of people who looks just like Jane. And there it is. Duh. Leah and Jane, hanging out together. Without me. Who are those other girls? And those guys?

"Marley? You have those balls?"

I walk back to the court. "Could we just pack up?" I say. "I'm done." Any spark of energy I may have had has been snuffed.

In my brain, I know there's nothing wrong with Leah and Jane hanging out with those Curtain Call people. But they made it sound like they had to be together to get all this work done. Really, they're just hanging out, having fun. Without me.

* * *

Thursday with the twins is another endless one. Grace skins her knee and refuses to go back outside. Faith won't come inside. I have to stand on the porch, with Grace right inside the front door. I must go in and out that door more than three hundred times.

Grace finally comes running outside, carrying two balloons with ribbons attached. Faith grabs them from her.

"Get off my balloon!" Grace screams, racing after her.

"Come and get it," Faith says.

"It's MINE!" Grace screams. "The pink one's mine! Give it!"

I can't tell if it's on purpose, but at that moment, Faith trips. Of course only one balloon gets loose. And starts soaring straight up to the sky.

It's pink.

"Noooooooooo!" Grace cries. "It was MINE!"

"Quick!" I say. *What, Marley? Quick, what?* I have their attention. What? "Make a wish, Grace!"

"Why?"

"You never heard of wishing on a balloon in the sky? Quick! It was your balloon, so it's your wish!"

Grace closes her eyes to think.

Faith lets go of her balloon too. She closes her eyes.

I want to go lie down somewhere and take a nap. For the rest of the summer.

* * *

By the time Dad picks me up, I feel like a capital-S Survivor. I have lived through a week of Grace and Faith, albeit a four-day week. The six twenty-dollar bills in my pocket are nice, but I'm pretty sure I'm being paid well below minimum wage, and I'm also sure that few workers on earth are more challenged by their daily job than I am.

I vow not to look ahead at all the five-day weeks remaining. I will just enjoy this time off, this three-day break. I hum the whole way home.

When I walk in the door, I grab a Diet Coke and sit on the couch with a book, ready to celebrate my freedom.

"Marley?" my dad says. "A little help?"

He so does not get me.

"Can't I just have a few minutes?" I say, not taking any care to hide my mega-annoyance.

"Just a little help and then I'll leave you alone."

"Fine."

Dad stands in front of some new towers of boxes that he neatly stacked in the corner of the living room. "I haven't figured out the trash collection days here yet, but if I get my garbage out there, sooner or later they'll have to take it."

Dad has always been the kind of guy who knows the trash collection schedule for the whole town. But of course, this is the new him. I just stare.

"So are you going to help?"

It's not bad enough my days are spent with

spit-bubble-blowing, balloon-releasing, whining five-year-olds; apparently I need to spend my free time carting cartons with my father.

"We need to bring out the ones from here to the street, and then we'll get the ones that are already in the garage."

"Didn't I already bring one of these out?"

"One? Yes, Marley. You did bring out one. Do you notice how many remain?"

"Well, Mr. Baird, sir. I'm not so good at math, sir. So, uh, no?"

He gives me a look. It disguises his love for me quite effectively. "Okay. Why don't you just take the ones from the garage out to the curb, and then you and Rig can go outside for a while. Please. Maybe at a great distance from where I can see you. I'll do the rest."

I haul eight boxes from the garage to the curb, placing the one with the Monopoly box on top of a big pile, the carton's flaps blowing in the light wind. Then I call for Rig and step out the back door to the yard. Jack is just standing there, staring at our house with a bizarre look on his face: almost cross-eyed, and very serious.

"I willed you to come out," he says.

"Whazat?" Oh, great. I'm talking like a twin.

"I didn't want to bug you. Were you guys doing something?"

I shake my head no.

"Do you want to take Rig for a walk or something?"

"That's exactly what I want to do," I say.

Jack nods. "Yes. I willed it to be."

"Is that face you were making a will-it-to-be face?"

He smiles. I realize then and there that the expression *weak in the knees* is an actual phenomenon.

I run back in to tell Dad where I'm going, all the while trying to name the weird feelings floating around my stomach and drifting up to my head. It's not that different from the way I feel at school when I have a crush on someone, always someone who has absolutely no idea, of course. But it *is* different. There's something that makes this more like its own flip side. Like instead of it being a mostly nervous, anxious feeling, this is closer to a slightly nervous, excited feeling.

As I step outside, Jack holds something up to show me. An old radio? "So we won't miss the game."

Game. The Yankees game. "Excellent," I say, feeling like a big liar. I could probably miss a season or two and not feel it too deeply.

"So," Jack says. "How was yesterday? Any easier?

Or did you find out there's a high-maintenance python you need to take care of too?"

"No, just twins. I don't mean to make it sound like a tough job. I mean, it's not hard like you have to be smart or strong or anything like that." *Shut up, Marley.*

A bizarre sound, like a coyote howl, distracts me. *Thank you, random coyote, for shutting me up.*

"The Williamsons," Jack says. "They have this chow-shepherd mix. Look upstairs, middle window of the green house."

I see a dark nose pushed against the screen window. The howling continues, loud.

It's soon joined by a higher-pitched bark: "Arah-rah! Arah-rah! Arah-arah-rah!" On the front porch of the next house is a poofy gray dog, turning in circles and yipping at Rig. "Arah-rah! Arah-rah!" Turn. "Arah-arah-rah!" Turn the other way.

"Real dog neighborhood, huh?"

"Yeah."

"There aren't many dogs where my mom lives. Down the street, there used to be this big white boxer, Beulah. She was Rig's best friend."

Jack gives me a look.

"What? Dogs can have best friends. Whenever I walked by their house, Beulah's owner, this old woman, would ask if Rig could play for a while. He'd bound into their yard and Beulah and Rig would both get up on their hind legs to greet each other, and then play like wild things."

Usually I can't make myself talk to someone new. Today I can't get myself to shut up.

"Dog best friends," Jack says.

"Yeah, but it's so sad. Beulah moved. Over a year ago. Every time we pass that house, I mean, like, almost every day, Rig just sits and stares, like he's waiting for an invitation to the backyard. I grab his collar and try to pull him along, but he just looks toward the yard. I'm not making this up. He gets that mournful puppy-dog look. It could break your heart."

"That's pathetic. Here, come this way." He turns down a street, away from the park I thought we were headed toward. Rig, out ahead of us a little, does an excellent dog double take—looking first where we're headed and then turning to look at me. He trots to catch up. Halfway down the street Jack turns again, this time onto a path. "I take this shortcut to camp."

It's really lush and beautiful, enchanted-forest-like, with ferns growing everywhere and big trees that meet in gentle arches overhead. We're walking underneath a tunnel of branches with sunshine shafting down in unexpected pools of light, and I think of Hansel and Gretel.

"Will Rig take off after a rabbit?" Jack asks. "I sometimes see them back here."

"No, he'll be fine. Unless, of course, the rabbits hang out with flies. Then he'll do his stotal paz fly dance."

"Stotal paz?"

"Oh, it's something my friend Jane always says. Sort of the supersize version of a total spaz."

"Right. Is that who was at your house the other day? Jane?"

"Yeah, Jane and Leah. They're my best friends. Since, like, forever." My brain keeps going back to the memory of them yesterday with those other kids, drawn to it the way my index finger always seeks the slightly painful beginnings of a hangnail on my thumb.

"Hey, there's one," Jack says, pointing at a rabbit sitting on top of an old tree stump.

I watch Rig go through his rabbit-spotting routine. He freezes, like a rabbit himself, and watches. The rabbit seems to sense Rig's presence and also goes completely still. Rig's body is rigid, his ears all perked up, eyes wide open. He's panting, and his tail is pointing straight out behind him, wagging slowly. Then he takes one leap—just one—toward the rabbit.

I always think that he's saying, *I could! I could chomp you with my big giant dog teeth! I could chase you! I could catch you! I could! Make sure you know that, rabbit! I could! I so could!*

Then he looks at me and his body totally relaxes. The doggy equivalent of *Just kidding.* He goes back to sniffing along the path. Something stinky must have been along before us, because he is one enthusiastic sniffer today, reaching back into the ferns growing in the deep shade, pushing under tall, thick grasses, then sniffing up, up the trunks of trees.

"So work's okay?"

"Well, those two little girls are sort of awful to each other. I always thought there was something special, like almost magical, about a twin. I thought it would be like a real, true best friend."

"Like you and your friends?"

"Um, maybe not exactly. Or yeah, maybe. I'm not sure."

"That's exactly what Will was like," Jack says. "He moved right before school ended. When we were little, his family always used to call us the twins."

The path ends, and I see that we're near the soccer field at the park, the very one my team used to play on when I was younger. "I never knew there was a path back here."

"Ah, there is much you have not yet learned, my friend."

I get a little jolt at that word, *friend*.

"You want to sit for a while?" Jack asks.

"Do you?" There is something so new here. It's like figuring out our own means of communication.

"We could keep walking."

"Sure."

Rig trots a little ahead so that we're following him again. "How long have you had Rig?"

"Since first grade."

"He's a great dog."

I know that this isn't just something he's saying; he gets it. When Leah and Jane come over, Rig runs over to greet them, barks his friendly "Ruh," with his tail wagging, and their hands go up around their faces, as far from him as they can possibly get. They don't hate him or anything. They just couldn't care less.

"Do you have a dog?" I ask. We're rounding the far side of the field, heading toward the playground and tennis courts that divide the soccer area from the base-ball fields.

"We did for a while, but my brother took her with him when he moved out. She's a golden retriever: Scout. She comes over every once in a while, when my brother comes to visit. I miss her a lot. I really miss having a dog."

"Why'd she go with your brother? Was she his dog?"

"Not exactly. She was a great dog. To me. She some-times bit people."

"Oh, that sucks. So how old's your brother?"

"Twenty."

"Are you close?"

"I don't know. We used to hang out a lot more, but he's been working really hard. You'd like him. A big fan. All year we save our money so we can buy a bunch of Yankees tickets the day they go on sale."

"So, Scout," I say. "Is that like a Boy Scout thing?"

"No, my mom named her for some girl in a movie. *To Kill a Mockingbird*. I sometimes think she wishes she had a daughter."

I'm about to tell him about Rig and the son my fa-ther never had, and maybe even clear up the big-time

Yankee fan confusion. Something else gets my attention.

I spot Leah's pink and yellow bike. I lean all the way to my right, try to see behind her, to see if Jane's there too, with a posse of new friends. If anyone else is with Leah, they're following at a great distance. She rides down the path and stops right in front of me. "OH! My God! Marley! Fancy meeting you here."

"Hey, Leah. How's it going?"

"It's been an amazing week. *Amazing!*" Her eyes lock on Jack, look up, look down. She shakes out her hair, her gorgeous, wavy honey brown hair.

"I had no idea CC was going to be so intense. It's, like, *so* intense! This week? We were working on character study because next week we're going to audition? And so Jane and me were up until, like, midnight and—"

It will be August before she's done if I don't stop her. I feel Jack next to me. "Do you guys know each other?" There's a sort of grunt of nonresponse from Jack. Then I say, "Leah, this is Jack. Jack, well, duh, this is Leah."

They smile at each other.

"So anyway, I'm sorry me and Jane haven't been around. We haven't had a minute when we're not rehearsing or practicing or whatever. We'll see you tomorrow, right? At Jane's." Then, to Jack she says, "It was really nice meeting you, Jack."

"See ya," Jack says. When Leah rides off, Rig turns his big head to watch, then looks back at us.

Jack walks over to a bench and sits right in the middle, then scoots over to the end a bit and motions for me to sit, too. Rig settles at our feet.

"She can be weird sometimes, but she and Jane are my best friends," I tell Jack, even though I've already told him. There's something almost defensive in my voice that doesn't make sense.

"Yeah, she seems cool," he says. He's quiet, just looking at me, and there are those eyes. His brown hair is a little shaggy, not a look I usually like. There's just something. I start to get all fluttery inside. Unable to talk.

An ugly tan pigeon lands on the back of the bench, a little too close to me. I think for a second about Elsie Jenkins, the monochromatic no-friends girl in her tan windbreaker. I wonder what people with no friends do all summer.

We sit there for a while, just looking around. Every time I look at Jack's face, really look at it, my stomach starts flipping. If I stopped to think about any of this, I doubt I could ever talk to him. I doubt I could walk. Or breathe without panting.

*   *   *

Back at our block, Jack says, "Let me know if you want to take a walk sometime."

"Yeah, I'll will you to come outside, okay?"

"Might work," he says. "Just don't forget to make the face. The face is key." He shows me the radio. "We forgot to listen to the game!"

"Man!" I stamp my foot to show my great displeasure. As he walks toward his house I'm pricked by the feeling that I have to come clean about that whole Yankee thing. It reminds me of opening the fridge at home and smelling something sour. My mother will always take out all the bottles and cartons, open each one, and sniff. I'll just shut the door and go into the pantry to find something else, but that sour smell lingers in my brain, worrying me.

The row of cartons neatly piled in front of Dad's house has doubled since I left. He's heading out with his arms full of more when he sees me. "Leah rode by," he says. "She said you saw her at the park."

"Yeah, I went with that kid who lives over there." I point toward Jack's house, trying not to let my face show the four hundred and fifty-seven emotions that scramble into play when I even think about him.

Dad smiles, a kind of surprised smile. "Jack Hadley?"

Hadley? I nod. "How do you know him?"

"He wasn't in my class, but I know him as a student at Little Valley. And sometimes I play catch with him." I knew that. I'd seen that. There's just something about hearing him *say* that. It's just so weird. He puts the pile of boxes down next to him on the lawn.

"He was in his yard the morning after I moved in, throwing high fly balls to himself," Dad says. "I called over and asked if he wanted to throw the ball around."

I think again about the son Dad never got to have. I always thought he'd appreciate someone to have catches with, go to games with, maybe wrestle or some other contact boy sport with. I get an image of my dad and Jack wrestling and my body involuntarily wiggles and jerks, trying to shake it away, to go back in time and not have to have that image ever even appear.

Rig looks up at me, then looks around, as though he's trying to find the very thing that gave me the willies so he can chase it away. He sees nothing, so he climbs the front steps and curls up, head near his tail, in front of the door.

"Jack and I saw Leah while we were in the park. Jack showed me a shortcut path to the soccer fields." Do I keep saying *Jack*? Why do I keep saying *Jack*?

"Now that you seem to be in a less horrifically teen-age mood, do you think you could give me a hand with the rest of the boxes? There aren't many left."

"I need to talk to you about something," I blurt out, reaching for one of the boxes. I'm scared, because Dad turns into this cartoony impatient old tortoise whenever things don't go smoothly, but I have to make him understand. Or this will be the worst and longest summer ever.

"Go right ahead," he says, still focused on the stacks of cartons.

"I want you to listen," I say. What I really want is for him to already know. Or to do what Mom always does, help me figure out a solution by talking the way normal people talk.

He finally stops what he's doing and looks at me. Well, that's something.

"This summer . . . it's not at all what I expected. I mean, I never thought I'd have to work every day, and—"

"We've been over this," Dad says, his hand up to stop me from going any further. "It's a done deal."

I take a deep breath. "And also, no computer? Can't we at least go to Mom's so I can use my computer here? One thing that could make my days a little more fun after working at a job I sure never asked for would be to at least be able to chat or be on Facebook or whatever. But—"

He shakes his head quickly like it doesn't matter. "I have no online connection anyway."

"Well, couldn't you get it?"

"This is the economic reality of a two-household family, Marley."

"What?" *In English, por favor.*

"We have to be careful with money. Your mother and I have the same income as we had before, but we're paying for two separate households now."

And whose brilliant idea was that, anyway?

"This whole thing just sucks," I say.

"It affects us all, Marley. Not just you."

I carry his stupid boxes out to the curb with the rest of the trash.

What Summer Should Be

I celebrate the Fourth of July by sleeping until the afternoon. Dad must have put Rig out early, because nothing wakes me until Dad opens my door and says, "If you keep sleeping, you'll miss the whole summer. It will be the first day of school."

I remember right away. Today is the day. Today is my day. Hey, world, all hail the soon-to-be Water Balloon Blitz all-time champ.

I take a fast shower, get dressed, and try to think about how to kill the time until I'm supposed to go to

Jane's. I call my mom. Amazingly, she actually answers her cell. But she starts rambling about reuniting with Yumi and Poodie and all these people (or, judging from the names, stuffed animals) I've never heard of. When she's finally done, she says, "So whose house this year for the Fourth?" I'm about to share my ingenious blitz plan when another call beeps in that Mom has to take.

I hang up and find Dad sitting at the kitchen table with the newspaper and a big cup of coffee.

It's tricky business when you don't feel like talking to someone, but he's the only other one in the house. The guy who ruined my summer is my only housemate.

"Morning," I say.

"Afternoon," he says.

"Thanks for letting me sleep."

"You are gifted at sleep, Marley. You always have been."

"I have many special talents," I say.

"What do you have planned for today?"

"Oh, I'm just going to Jane's. You know, same old Fourth of July stuff. Some friends from their class are coming, too, I think." I don't mention that Jane's locking her parents inside the house or whatever. They'll be nearby, and that's enough. Dad doesn't need to know everything.

"That curtain class?" Turns out Dad really doesn't know anything. Does he picture Leah and Jane, maybe wearing bonnets, bent over old sewing machines?

"Curtain Call, yeah. What are you doing?"

"I may go fishing," Dad says, "unless you want me to wait for the weekend, so we can go together."

"No, you should go today," I blurt, a little too fast. Then, to distract him, I ask, "Can you take me to Jane's?"

"What time?"

I look at the big coffee cup clock. "Around four."

"Okay. Or you could ride your bike there and I'll pick you up later."

"Yeah, okay." I say. It's a long ride, but I guess it'll help pass the hours.

Summer's supposed to be about all this delicious, lazy time, and I can't help noticing that I'm either waiting for it to pass so I can do something good, or I'm counting off the minutes until the worst part of my day—the twin part—is over. No. I'm not thinking twins now. No way.

I need to go online, check my e-mail and stuff. I should go to the library, but no, it's closed on the Fourth. Maybe I can do it at Jane's tonight.

"Come on, Rig," I say. I take my book and bring

him into the backyard. I like the backyard. That definitely has something to do with its proximity to someone else's yard, but even if there were no Jack, I think I'd like it back here. I take a deep delight in the fact that my father has a totally weedy lawn. It makes me think anything is possible.

I'm just sitting on an old aluminum chair in the yard, reading. It's quiet. Rig is lying by my side. I realize it's the most relaxed, comfortable moment I've had this summer. I'm not tired. I don't have to face twins today or tomorrow or even the next day. I'll be hanging out with my best friends in a little while. I'm about to have them bow down before me, about to win their undying Water Balloon Blitz Respect. There's also the matter of a guy. He lives in that house over there, and I think about him from time to time. Or all the time.

I wonder what he thinks of me. Am I just some nearby person, some Yankees fan with an excellent dog, who moved into a house that's near his house?

I finish my book and set it down on the grass right next to a huge dandelion cluster. I reach to pull it out and I'm sort of wrestling with it—it has really deep roots—when I hear Jack calling my name.

"Hey, Jack!" I yell back.

"What are you doing?"

"Oh, nothing. What are you doing?"

"I mean with the grass. You look like you're fighting with the lawn. And maybe losing."

"Just trying to pull something out. No camp today?"

"On the Fourth? No. Just hanging. You?"

"Yeah, for now."

"You want to watch the fireworks later?"

Oooh! Yes, I do. More than he could possibly even come close to imagining.

But Leah and Jane and I have a code of friendship that prohibits us from canceling plans with each other for some guy.

But before, it was always just the *idea* of some guy. This is *Jack*. He's more than some guy. It's not as if Leah and Jane even invited me along when they—

But no. No. You don't treat your friends like that. You don't.

Oh! I want to! I want to cancel.

Speak, Marley. "I'm supposed to go to Jane's house," I say.

"Oh, okay. You're around this weekend, though?"

"Yeah," I say.

I want to say more. I hate not getting to be with him. What can I say?

"Have fun. I'll see ya."

"Yeah. See you later."

* * *

"Bye, Dad. I'll call you when I'm ready to come home, okay? Probably sometime after the fireworks." Jane's house is on a hill, so even though she's not that near the park, she has a great view.

"Have fun, Marley. Be careful."

"I always am."

I have that prickly it's-my-birthday kind of pins-and-needles feeling. This is going to be so fun! Stealing the title back from Leah!

It's a hot day, but I love creating my own cool breeze as I cruise from this part of town back to my real neighborhood. It brings back the days when Leah and Jane and I finally got our bicycle independence and were allowed to ride around the neighborhood together, without a parent. We were giddy with freedom. We have so much history like that.

I go four blocks out of my way to ride down my street. I don't have my keys with me, but I'd love to go inside. To just look at my desk. To sit in front of my bookcase stacked with all my old favorites. When I think of what I really want to be doing, my mind travels back a few miles to Jack. I'd like to just sit with Jack and look up at the sky.

I ride up Jane's driveway and place my bike neatly next to the garage. Jane's parents are kind of uptight— as if neatness matters more than comfort or having fun. If you ever forget where you are for a second and actually walk on their bright green lawn, Mr. or Mrs. Martin will run to the front door or pop out from a window to start squawking at you. My father considers their lawn a crime against nature. He says nothing could be that green without tons of toxic chemicals.

I tap my pocket, glad to hear the plastic rustling in there. I love this kind of secret, like when you've gotten the perfect gift for someone and just can't wait to give it to them. Only better. Bigger.

I ring the doorbell and Jane's right there. Jane-in-glasses. I hide my secret smile. "Hey!" she says. "Leah, she's here. Happy Fourth of July, Marley."

"Thanks so much," I say. "I had a lot to do with our country achieving independence, and it's good of you to remember that."

"Marley's here?" I hear, and then Jane's little sisters

and brother come running. It's not like I've ever been nice to them, but for some reason they love me.

"Hey, Christian. Hi, Sammi. I like your haircut, Josie."

"Mom!" Jane yells. "Can you please get them out of here?"

"Marley, how nice to see you," Mrs. Martin says, coming into the hallway, carrying a big grocery bag. Leah's walking behind her, carrying two bags of chips. "How are your parents?"

"My mom's away. I'm staying at my dad's. They're fine."

"Oh, well. Good. Tell them both I send my best."

"I will."

"As you have no doubt heard, we are all under strict orders to remain inside the house during this party. But if you need anything, please let me know. Are you sleeping over too?"

I shake my head. "Um, no. My dad's going to get me later." *Sleeping over? Too?*

"Well, have fun."

"Yeah, Mom. Stay inside. And make sure Sammi doesn't sneak out."

Leah grabs my arm and she and Jane lead me out

back. "OH! My God, Marley. We invited all the guys from our division and we told them to bring their friends and—"

"Your mom didn't flip?" I ask Jane.

"She knows we invited some people, but maybe not as many as we really did."

They will be right inside. What parent wouldn't look through a window? It's funny, because Jane's glasses really make her *look* smarter . . .

"What should I do?" I ask.

"Find the soda, and let's bring that tub over there outside, and throw whatever ice we have in it. Sage is going to bring some bags of ice, but that'll do until he gets here."

"Sage is coming?" I say, a smile creeping across my face. I love watching Jane when she's with a guy she likes. She gets so . . . tight. Leah is a natural flirt. When it comes to guys, Jane is more like me. She gets all stiff and shy.

I say I'm going to hunt down some more plastic cups, but I go back inside and race up to the second floor to scout a good water balloon launch site. The hall bathroom is perfect. Oh, yes. *Perfect*. What more could I ask for? Water source and best launching spot to the pool all in the same little room!

I rush back, with cups, so my absence isn't too obvious. We take armloads of towels outside to the little shed Mrs. Martin set up years ago, a place for swimmers to change out of their suits so they don't trek in and drip unwanted water in her house. Doing anything even remotely messy at Mrs. Martin's house takes incredible courage. I should be off the charts for Water Balloon Blitz Bonus Points. *The world welcomes its new champion, Marley Baird. Thank you. Thank you. Please, no photos at this time.*

I'm pouring a tub of pretzels into a big bowl when two guys and a girl show up. I can tell from the greetings that one of them is Sage, but Jane doesn't get around to introducing me. Jane! She has different glasses on now—they're just like her new glasses, only they're dark sunglasses. Wow.

The party revs up fast; each time I look around, there are more people. I thought there were only twenty people in their class, but those friends must have invited a lot of friends too, because the pool is pretty full and there are people all over the yard.

There are only one or two somewhat familiar faces besides Leah and Jane. No one I really know. Definitely no one who knows me. Leah and Jane are both talking in big groups of people who all seem to know each other, so I walk around, just trying to find a place for myself. I spot some bags of ice near the shed and pour all the ice into the tub. I shove the soda down deep so it'll get cold.

Well, then. I look around to make sure no one's watching me. No one is. I sneak into the house. It sounds like Jane's family is watching a movie—a pretty loud one—in the family room, in the front of the house.

I take my time in the upstairs bathroom. I'm like a surgeon preparing for a big operation, only without all the major hand and arm scrubbing. Balloons to the left of the sink. Cleared area by the window, on the bath mat, for filled ones. Deep breaths. Calm demeanor.

Balloon number one, yellow, attached to faucet with the ease of a pro. Slow flow. Inflate, wait.

I am a Water Balloon Blitz poet.

Tie knot.

I overfill a blue one and it ends up with this weird bulge. I push at the bulge and it disappears, but not really, because another bulge, same shape and size, shows up on the other side of the balloon. There's no hiding your bulges when you're a water balloon.

The first two are a little overfull—they'll break easily. You can tell by the feel when you've filled a water balloon exactly right. After the first few, I hit that just-right level each time.

I'm close to bursting with the complete and total awesomeness of what I'm about to pull off.

I stop to take stock—I have a lot. Like, the best stash ever. I open the window and pause, waiting for Jane's mother to start squawking. It's as if she has some freakishly programmed computer that tells her when to scream at someone for opening a window when the air conditioning is on. If she even saw the huge pile of water balloons on her bathroom floor, her computer would short-circuit and she would, well, probably drop dead. Painlessly and instantly.

Good. Silence. Except for happy pool noises: splash . . . squeal . . . laugh.

There are so many people here. They will all look up, figure it all out, and laugh until they can't breathe. Finally, Leah will shrug with a smile, like, "I can't compete with that!" And Jane will race up here to find my stash and get me back.

This isn't even going to be hard. I have the easiest angle in the world. Straight down is fine—straight out is fine. It's almost too easy.

I wish I could share this moment with someone. I love this!

I should post this on YouTube.

It's loud out there. I think about shouting a warning, but a blitz is a blitz—total shock factor required.

Ready, set, BLITZ! I'm barely breathing, just reaching and throwing, grabbing, throwing. It gets quiet, then people start shouting. I can't hear what they're saying, because I'm blitzing, baby! Yellow! Blue! Splash! Splash! Hands are going up over heads. Red! Yellow! Splash! One on the planter—whoops! People are looking up. I'm more than halfway through my stash. Splash! A rainbow one! Splash! Orange! Red! Splash! I'm going at it two-handed. I feel like I have four hands, I'm moving so fast.

I hear and feel what seems like a stampede of feet up the stairs, racing feet, like the house is on fire. "OH! My God, Marley. What the hell is the matter with you?" Leah is screaming. She grabs my hands at the window and makes me drop the balloons inside, splashing water all over the bathroom floor.

"What are you, like, FIVE?" Leah screams.

Jane walks into the room silently. Her face has gone completely white.

She looks embarrassed in the worst way imaginable. And totally, thoroughly pissed.

Like I showed up for her party naked and crapped in her pool.

She doesn't say a word.

I don't have a voice. I am speechless.

"Go outside," Leah says to Jane. "I'll take care of this."

Jane stares at me like I am someone she has always hated. Then she leaves the room. Leah continues the silence, shaking her head, a seriously, gravely disappointed parent.

"I was . . ." I start. But I stop. Because all at once, something pops inside of me.

I have made a huge and terrible and hideous mistake.

Leah rolls her eyes and says, "Just . . . never mind, Marley. Just go outside."

I am deadened. I numb-walk my way slowly back outside.

Everyone is in the pool; you can hardly even see the water for all the people. Jane is in the middle of everything, tossing a ball, screaming, laughing. She's no longer seething with fury and hate. Or at least she hides it well.

What can I do? What should I do? It comes to me

slowly. Whenever we have a . . . not a fight, but some kind of problem, we somehow move past it. We act normal, like nothing happened, and before too long it's just us, hanging out, together, back in the groove, past the problem. We push past it by refusing to be anything other than regular, the three of us, same as always.

I look around at the teen-movie party scene. This won't be easy.

When Leah comes back outside, she won't look at me. I walk near her. Twice. It's not like I'm invisible. It's worse. Like there's some seal around them I can't get through. I stare at Jane, but I can't see past those sunglasses.

I walk over to the shallow end and sit with my feet in the water. I feel people whispering behind me. I can almost feel them pointing. I see broken balloon pieces around the pool and think about picking them all up, hiding the evidence, pretending none of this happened, but I can't stand the thought of being seen picking up a balloon piece. The idea that everyone will know it was me.

Concentrate on feet in pool, Marley. Just think about the pool.

It's always eighty degrees in the Martins' pool, which is probably why it was always one of my happiest places to be. My July and August days at Jane's have always been as lazy and long as summer itself used to be. Even when Jane's little sisters and brother were in the pool with us, it was always my idea of what summer should be.

I hear two girls laughing behind me. I guess it could be about anything. But I know it's about me.

It's the Fourth of July and it's all wrong. All that lock-the-parents-in-the-house-and-invite-over-hundreds-of-people has turned this into some kind of reality show instead of my annual tradition with my best friends.

A loud group arrives, four guys, drinking from brown bottles that must contain beer, yelling, "Par-tay! Par-tay!" like they're at a frat house or something, and I'm thinking that they'd better shut up if they don't want Jane's neighbors to hear or her parents to come storming out of the house. I'm also thinking that my father would absolutely kill me, kill me dead and then a little more for good measure, if he knew what was going on here. Parents locked in the house. Older guys. Beer.

I see the beer guys pass a bottle to the tall guy in the chair by the pool. Great. A drunk lifeguard. That's what was missing.

There is no place for me here. I think about wading into the pool, but I need to stay away from Jane, who's still having a ball and still not looking at me. They're all involved in some intricate game with rules that are so not obvious to me. There seem to be teams, numbers called, a riot of shouts, then laughter and a splash. I walk around the pool, staying away from broken balloons, checking on the snacks, avoiding Leah, who is not looking at me the same way Jane is. One of the bowls of chips has tipped and I go inside to get a trash bag. I don't know if Mrs. Martin would be more mad about the way a few friends coming over to swim morphed into a crazed crowd in her yard (or has she been peeking out and is okay with this?) or an onslaught of hungry ants. Or the rubbery remnants of smashed water balloons. I can't help myself. I start to pick them up, then feel people looking at me, whispering. Talking. Like, *There's that freak who threw the water balloons from the second floor.*

I toss the trash and sit on one of the chaises closest to the pool, just watching and feeling something way worse than lonely, right here in the middle of all these people. It doesn't bother them, though. They all seem to be having a great time. I'll bet this is *their* idea of what summer should be.

Except for that weird Monopoly afternoon a few days ago, it's been so long since Leah and Jane and I just hung out. Even when we were together toward the end of school, it wasn't always great. When I tried to tell them how strange everything was after my dad moved out, I could never get the words right. I never felt like they got it.

And now. Now I've really screwed everything up. There's never been anything like this—both of them mad at me. What am I supposed to do?

Why did I think the blitz would be great? What an idiot. What an incredible idiot.

"Marley!" someone says. I can't see for the glare of the sun, so I'm squinting, wondering if it's Jane or Leah, since they're the only ones I know, except this voice doesn't have any hate in it.

I lower my head so I can look up at an angle. "Callie? Callie Larson?!" It seems almost miraculous that there's someone here willing to look at me. To talk to me. Hallelujah.

"My *LitMag* buddy!"

"My *LitMag* pal! What are you doing here?"

"My boyfriend goes to Curtain Call with Jane," she says.

"Who's your boyfriend?"

"Ethan Franks. You know him?" I shake my head. "Yeah, he goes to Little Valley."

"Cool," I say.

"How come you're not swimming?" she asks.

One cannot simply describe or explain today. "Not in the mood," I say, single-handedly winning the Understatement of the Year Award.

"Me neither." We sit and watch the action in the pool for a while. I feel a tiny bit less like the girl with the raw red rash all over her body, sitting with Callie. True, we're quiet and watching. But we're quiet and watching together, which lessens the loser factor. And I like Callie!

"So what have you been doing?"

"Not much. I've been stuck watching my little brother a lot, which totally sucks."

People line up at the diving board. As they jump, the others scream encouragement or low-grade ridicule, depending on the dive and the person.

Jane does a graceless cannonball that earns her a huge round of applause from the people in the pool. For a thin person, she makes an impressive splash.

Two guys jump off together. One right after the other. I'm scared someone's going to get hurt. Shouldn't the drunk lifeguard be stopping them? I stop watching for a while, instead just listening to the cheers and jeers. When I hear Leah say, "Watch me, you guys," I look up. She does some goofy sideways dive. Then it's totally silent.

I look around. One of the girls I don't know is elbowing another and rolling her eyes, but it seems like no one else is paying any attention.

I start clapping. "Good one, Leah!" I yell. Callie claps too.

Leah looks our way before swimming to the shallow end.

* * *

When the sun goes behind the trees that line the yard, people get out of the pool and start hanging in small groups on the chaises, at the tables, in the hammock. The outdoor lights come on. Jane's on Sage's lap in the back by the fence. It's weird, because she doesn't look at all stiff and uncomfortable. She looks like she's just where she wants to be, her fingers in his longish black hair. His hand is at the bottom of her back. I try to make eye contact with her; I need to apologize. She won't look my way.

Callie goes off with her boyfriend, so I scan the yard for Leah. I finally spot her moving around, going from group to group—not staying with anyone for too long. I watch her with one group of guys—she actually gets herself in the middle of their loose circle. Yup!

There it is. Her trademark. The Leah Stamnick Casual Arm Touch. Sometimes she claims she's not even flirting, that it's just the way she is, really touchy-feely. I'm not sure I believe that.

But even the Casual Arm Touch is failing to get her noticed. This is unprecedented. I grab two sodas from a tub and walk over to her just as she's walking away from that group. I try to hand her one but she doesn't take it. Finally, she puts her hand on her hip and asks, "What, Marley?"

"Listen," I say. "I'm so sorry. That was so stupid. I thought it would be funny, but it was just the worst idea."

"Is there a word that means 'worse than worst,' because really, I think that's the word you're looking for."

"Thank you?"

"OH! My God, Marley. Jane is so pissed."

"I know. I have to apologize, but she won't even look at me."

Leah looks around, and I can't help but assume that she's worried that people will see her standing with the loser. How can everything change so fast?

I start walking and pull Leah's arm. "Come with me. I need to apologize."

"Just wait. Not now."

"Now. I swear, this is bad, this is so bad, and I need to make it better. Like, now."

Leah looks at me, and though there's not a lot of friendliness in her eyes, she does give a shrug of understanding. Or something like that. "Wait here. I'll get her."

So I just stand there, like the world's biggest loser. Forever.

But forever, it turns out, is not long enough. Because what's coming at me looks fierce. Leah's face just looks blank, but Jane! Jane could kill people with the meanness on her face.

I look for courage. When I fail to find any, I remind myelf that we have always been friends and that this is the only way to fix it. I force myself to start talking. "Look, I'm sorry about before. That was a really bad idea. With the balloons. I screwed up. I thought it would be funny. It wasn't. It so wasn't. I'm really, really sorry."

"God, Marley! Do you know how long I planned this party? How hard I worked? I can't believe I even invited you. You just completely ruined it. This will always be the party when . . . Uch, I can't believe you."

She is shouting at me.

Everyone is staring.

Jane lowers her voice. Now she is hissing at me. "Did you really think we were going to be having little water balloon fights? Or maybe sit around playing Monopoly all night? I mean, aren't you ever going to grow up?"

I think I have stopped breathing.

I do not know where to look.

I somehow find the strength to turn my head and look to Leah. She heard Jane. She heard the meanness. Shouldn't that set off some alarm, some realization that people don't talk to their friends like that?

Leah catches my eye for only a second, an accidental second, before looking away.

I walk to the driveway and get my bike. There's still enough light in the sky for me to find my way home.

Fireworks in Miniature

A blast of sound vibrates the ground and startles me so much, I almost lose my balance. It takes longer than it should for me to realize the fireworks have started. Once I get used to the light and sound explosions, it's kind of nice to have something to entertain me and keep the sky lit as I make my way back home.

I push away all thought and concentrate on my legs, pushing pedals, getting home. I do not think about the Water Balloon Blitz Disaster. I do not think about how much I do not like my friends. I do not even go near wondering who my friends are if they're not Leah and Jane. I just pedal. Pedal. Pedal.

I put the bike in the garage and walk into the house. Dad's on the phone, so I just mouth *I'm home*. He gives me a look saying he didn't expect me. Rig spots me and comes trotting over for his long-lost-friends-reunited-at-last greeting. "Come on outside," I say, and walk out the back door.

Rig races out faster than usual. "Hey there, Rig," I hear from the other side of the hedges. "Hey."

"Jack?" I say.

"Marley?"

"Yeah."

"I thought—"

"Long story."

"Well, I have time. You wanna see something?"

"What?"

"Just take a walk with me."

"Let me tell my dad."

I run back in the house. He's still on the phone. I mouth, *Taking a walk*. He nods.

Jack leads Rig and me to the front of his house, then we head down the block. The night keeps going dark and then lighting up again. I keep thinking the fireworks are over when another set lights up the sky.

He stops in the middle of an empty lot. The rest of the street is filled with houses and yards, and here's this random empty, undeveloped spot, marked out in a long rectangle by trees around the property line.

"What's the deal with this?" I ask him.

"My father says it's about fire access, some kind of reason they couldn't build anything here. Look. There it is."

He points up. There, on top of a tree, is an old tree house for kids, with dirty signs out front saying KEEP OUT and PRIVATE PROPERTY.

"Shall we?" he asks, pointing to the ladder up the back.

I hate to be the voice of reason, but I have to ask. "Is this trespassing?" More than that, I'm thinking, *You? Me? Up there? Just us?*

"My brother helped me and Will build it. It's ours. Well, mine now, I guess."

"Who's Will?"

"He was my best friend, remember? The one who moved away."

"Did he live nearby?"

"Very," Jack says. "In the house your dad moved into." He looks so sad.

Oh no. NO! Here come those tears again. I've been

so good for days! I cannot cry in front of Jack. Poor Jack lost his best friend. And poor me. I'm not sure if I even like my best friends anymore. And I'm absolutely certain they don't like me.

"Will and I used to watch the fireworks from here every year."

I step ahead of Jack and climb the ladder that's nailed to the tree's trunk. When the sky brightens from a flurry of white light, I try not to think about Jack staring at the backs of my legs.

Rig starts to whine. "Just wait down there," I tell him. He circles the tree twice, then settles down, his head resting on a small bump of tree root. I think of Rig staring at Beulah the boxer's house. Is that how Jack feels when he's looking at Dad's house? Is he really willing me out or just longing for Will?

It's dirty in the tree house, disintegrated-leaf dirty. It smells like old rot. "What did you guys do up here?"

"Guy stuff," Jack says. My brain has an image, all at once, of little boys playing pirates, on the lookout for land; of baseball cards in a pile; comic books traded back and forth; marbles. What about when they were older?

"Like what kind of guy stuff?"

"I could tell you," Jack says. "Sadly, I'd then have to kill you. Sorry."

"Hmm," I say. "You don't sound sorry."

He shrugs. "Nothing I can do about it. Guy Code secret."

I wonder if Guy Code is anything like our code. I'm pretty sure my friends did not honor the unwritten rules of friendship tonight. Oh, God, no. Tonight.

"So what do you think of the joint?" Jack asks, smiling. I sit down before I can register how weak in the knees I feel. That smile has an effect on me that is not like anything that's come before. I sit down with my back against the wall. Jack sits against the wall to my left. Our sneakers are touching.

My crushes have always been intense, but wholly one-way. With Jack, it feels like there's a possibility that this might be a two-way street. Couldn't he be interested in me too?

I want to ask him, *So are we going to do guy stuff?* but it sounds like a come-on. I wish I could bring myself to brush his arm with a trademarked Leah Stamnick Casual Arm Touch or let my sneakered foot play with his.

"So what's the deal with that camp, anyway? Are you like a counselor? Or—"

"There's no name for what I am. I don't pay to go. They don't pay me. I'm just . . . in the middle. I help out. I love it there."

I look up at the wall. There's a poster of the Yankees team from six years ago on one wall, and another listing all their championships next to it. He sees me looking. "Will was a Yankees fan too," he says. "Your house is destined to be occupied by Yankees fans. It has been decreed."

I could just casually mention that maybe I'm not as big a Yankees fan as he thinks I am. But if I like talking about the Yankees with Jack, and I do—I like talking about everything with him—then maybe it's okay?

"Where does Will live now?"

"South Carolina."

"Oh. That's far."

"We thought we'd visit each other a lot, but so far we've talked on the phone a little and done some IMing. I don't know. So what about you?"

"What?"

"You said you had some long story about tonight. About why you're home now instead of with your friends."

"Oh, just this thing."

"What kind of thing?"

"A bad thing."

"Some kind of fight?"

"No, not a fight. I don't know. They had this party

with some new friends and . . . I don't know. I'm sure it'll be okay." I don't really believe the words I just said. I can't imagine any way this can all work out. But we've always been friends. It never occurred to me that could ever change. Those friendships have been a fact of my life, as true as math. But right now it's turned into an equation I cannot begin to figure out.

"Were they acting like—"

"Jerks? Kind of. Yeah."

"I get pissed when people treat me bad. If you're going to be my friend, you need to always treat me right, you know? I can't stand it when people are jerks. I don't need that."

That's it. I can't say it, but that's exactly it. I do need them. They're my best friends. They've always been my best friends. Tonight, though, he's right. They didn't act that way. I'm sure they think that what I did was even worse.

"It just wasn't a great party," I say. "I didn't know anyone and I sort of felt like a loser." *No. Stop talking, idiot. Do not tell him about the Water Balloon Blitz Disaster.*

"So what'd you do?"

"After making a complete fool of myself by throwing water balloons out the window onto the people at the party?" *Marley! Hey, Marley? Shut up!*

His face! He's silent-laughing, like he can't believe what I'm saying. "Should I even ask what you did next?"

"I left."

"Well, at least that was smart."

"I guess." I wonder what they said when I left. Do they hate me? I'm not wild about them right now, but it's not like I meant to throw away my two best friends, either.

I hate feeling like a fool. I felt so brave when I was up in that bathroom, in pre-Blitz mode. I wonder if brave and stupid are sometimes a little too close to each other.

Talking about stuff like this with Jack, that takes some courage too. Only I'm not sure how much more of that I have. Or if I should trust my judgment to know when I'm being brave and when I'm being stupid. I'm not at all sure I know the difference.

We're quiet for a while. I don't know if he feels it too, but it's almost as if there are some warm, delicious sparks flying, Fourth of July fireworks in miniature, right here in this tree house.

I wonder what it says about me that I'm more comfortable in a little kids' tree house with a guy I've known for less than a week than I was at a party with my best friends since second grade.

Nasty Princesses That Knock Down Stuff

M y dad insists that we play tennis before dinner on Tuesdays and Thursdays, the two slow days for his lawn care business. I complain like crazy in the beginning, but the truth is, tennis helps to pass the time. It keeps me from checking my cell phone every other minute. Is it working? Do I have messages? Why don't I have messages? How can this be happening?

I have bad days on the court and good days, like always, but it does seem that the more we play, the fewer bad days there are. On one of the bad days, when I'm gathering up all the balls I've hit into the bushes, I see Leah and Jane out with their Curtain Call friends.

I would have thought that the stunning shock of a pain like this would wane, but it's still raw, like new. Leah's the easiest to spot, as that awful yellow and pink bike would stand out anywhere. Also, she's the only one on a bike, as if everyone decided at once that they don't ride bikes anymore only no one remembered to tell Leah. There's a guy who I think is Sage, and two other girls. It seems as though Jane and Sage are a little off by themselves. I don't know if they see me, but if they do they don't let on.

It keeps getting worse. Or maybe I'm just now realizing how bad it is. What have I done? I didn't know when I left that party that I'd have to give up everything. I can't just let go of all those years, the two best friendships. Every time I'm about to reach for the phone, to check my messages one more time or maybe even to call them, I stop.

I get to the point, finally, when I stop checking messages. I don't even bother charging my phone; it's not like anyone's calling me, and it gets kind of depressing to see that I've missed zero calls.

Jack and I spend more time together. Even when

we're not together, I'm thinking about him. A lot. Wondering if he thinks about me.

We talk every morning before he heads out to camp, and he wills me out after work each day. We walk Rig, hang out up in the tree house, and mostly, we talk. We talk about baseball camp and the twins, the Yankees, his parents and mine, and how little we're looking forward to school in the fall.

For him, fall is all about sports, which team he might make. He's nervous about flubbing the tryouts for some new travel team. I make it seem as if my own complete lack of enthusiasm is just about the whole idea of going back to school. That's not really it. I know exactly what I'm anxious about. How do you start school without friends? I wonder if I should go buy my Elsie Jenkins limited edition tan windbreaker now.

I'd probably lie awake each night worrying about it, but my weekdays are a new kind of thoroughly exhausting physical torture. As the twins get to know me more, they want to do more. When I come over, they have lists of all they want to do that day. Lynne says they spend their whole night asking her how to spell words so they can write them down. After three days of "GO 2 PARK" at the top of the list, I get the hint.

Lynne drops us in the parking lot behind the playground. "What time would you like me to pick you up, Marley? I'd like to let the baby sleep a bit. Is one thirty too late?"

"That's fine," I say.

"Let's eat first!" Grace says.

"Dessert first!" Faith says. "Kwee have dessert, Marley?"

"No. We're going to play in the playground for a while, and then we'll have a picnic lunch."

"A picnic?"

"Yes."

"I love picnics."

"Excellent."

And then, at the same instant, like twin bunnies, they take off toward the swings. "Marley! Marley! Push me!" Grace calls.

I walk behind the swings and push Grace. I'm about to push Faith too, but she screams. "Don't! I'm pumping!"

She's a good pumper, too. It took me a long time to get the hang of pumping—I thought it was just a leg-motion thing. Watching Faith, I see the way she works her whole body and gets the swing rocking higher and higher. Grace bends her legs out/in, out/in, but she doesn't gain any height from it. I give her big pushes.

The girls are calm, concentrating on getting higher, higher. In the quiet I catch the metallic sound of a bat hitting a ball, over and over.

"Push me higher, Marley!" Grace reaches out with her legs, trying to pump. "Higher!"

"You are such a baby, Grace. You always need pushes."

"So what?"

"So you're a baby."

"You are."

Faith is pumping herself even higher than I can push Grace. As Faith's swing nears the top of its frontward arc, she jumps off.

"Whoa," I say, relieved she didn't break her neck. What am I supposed to do if she breaks her neck?

"Bet you couldn't never do that, Baby Grace." Faith takes off to the ladder for the high slide.

Grace is trying not to cry. I push her as high as I can, hoping to cheer her somehow.

I ask, "Do you ever pretend not to hear her? That might really drive her crazy."

"She don't care," Grace says. "Stop me, Marley. I wanna go with Faith now."

I grab the chains and slow the swing. I can't tell if she is really hurt by the things her sister says or if this is just how they are. I'm not even sure it's my business. Shouldn't the parents be dealing with this stuff?

Grace waits until the swing has completely stopped swaying, then steps lightly off. As soon as she hits the ground, though, she is off, racing hard toward her sister.

They meet up at the slide, where they take turns getting up the ladder and then going down the slide a different, goofy way. They do it over and over and over. Down feet-first on their back, headfirst on their side, each trying to outdo the other one for silliness.

I stand on one of the benches to see if I can glimpse the baseball fields from here, but there are too many trees in the way. I sit back and try to pick sounds out. It's impossible, aside from the odd *ping* and general loud shouts. The twins are laughing loud, and the baseball field is too far away.

Faith starts climbing up the slide when Grace is about to go down, and Grace, without a word, starts crying.

"Faith, come on," I say. "You know you go *up* the ladder and *down* the slide."

She gets this look on her face that I've learned the

meaning of. If five-year-olds had a good cursing vocabulary, this look would translate to one of the worst words. She just sits in the middle of the slide, one foot touching each side. She is not moving.

Grace decides to go down anyway, and she picks up some speed before banging into her sister. They tumble off at the bottom, hands and feet all tangled. I hear Grace's high-pitched yelp and race over.

They look at me at the same time. Grace's eyes are still red from crying, but I can see now that she's laughing. "Kwee do that again, Marley Bear?"

"No. Try to come up with some different way to nearly kill each other."

"Okay."

Faith runs to the monkey bars and effortlessly walks her way, hand over hand, across the length. Grace tries to follow, but her hands can't hang on; she's down on the ground after two bars.

The minute Grace clears out from underneath, Faith races across again, this time stopping in the middle to put her feet to the bar, an upside-down bridge. Then she drops her legs back down and makes her way across, hand over hand.

I can see Grace's frustration. She looks like she's going to walk over to Faith and kick her or pull her hair out of her head. "Anybody want to take a walk before our picnic?" I say in a ridiculous Mary Poppins voice.

"Walks are boring."

"I don't want to."

"If you take a short walk with me, I'll let you eat your dessert first when we get back."

" 'Kay," Grace says.

Faith steps to my side and puts a hand in mine. "Walks are great," she says.

"Let's see what's on the other side of those tennis courts," I say. "Maybe there's something interesting."

"Haven't you never been there?" Grace asks.

"I don't think so. Have you?"

"We been all over this park. Our daddy took us here," Faith says.

Grace adds, "He used to."

"Yeah?"

"We'd ride our bikes sometimes. Tricycles and training wheels. And I'm ready for my training wheels to come off, but Mommy says—"

"I know, Faith."

"Mommy says that even when we were little babies, they'd take us for rides here," Grace says. "They had little seats they put on their bikes so they could ride us around. We'd just sit there. I think it must have been fun, getting riddened all around with someone else doing the riding. I'm so hungry, Marley. Kwee go back for dessert now?"

"We just started walking. Let's keep going until we can see what they're doing over there. It sounds like there's a lot of kids playing."

Actually, it's gone quiet. It must be lunchtime or something. I wonder what kind of lunch was in Jack's swinging baseball bag this morning.

I see a few people now, littler kids mostly, sitting on benches with lunch boxes open on their lap and next to them. "Kwee just eat our dessert when we get back, Marley Bear? Do we have to eat the lunch too?"

"Well?" Grace asks.

"Marley Bear!" Faith says.

"Lunch too," I say. "Let's just walk a little farther first."

Finally I see Jack walking in from the outfield, carrying four or five canteens on his shoulder. He calls out, "Which of you geniuses left your water out in the sun?"

I hear a round of "Sorry, Jack!" and "Thanks, Jack," and "Oops! That one's mine. Thanks!"

He's walking over to deliver a Snoopy thermos on a strap to a kid on a bench directly in front of us when he sees me. "Marley!" he says, a big smile on his face. "And let me see, which one of you is Grace?"

"Duh," Faith says. "Her."

I wish I were allowed to kick her. Just every now and then. Not all the time—that would be wrong. "Be nice, Faith. This is Jack."

"Hi," Grace says. "Marley's gonna let us eat our dessert first today because we went for a walk with her."

"She sounds like an awesome babysitter," Jack says.

"I don't know," Faith says.

"So this is where the camp is, huh?" It's lame, but it's all I can force out of my mouth.

"Kwee walk back for our dessert picnic now, Marley Bear?"

"I thought your last name was Baird, with a *d*."

"It is."

"She's really like a bear. 'Specially when she's mad."

"Yeah? And is she mad at you a lot?"

"Not a lot," Grace says.

"Yup, a lot," Faith says.

"What are you guys doing here?"

"We was playing in the playground and my sister was showing off on the monkey bars and then Marley Bear said we should take a walk and so now we're taking a walk."

"Sounds good," Jack says. I wonder if he thinks I steered them over here on purpose. I mean, I totally did, but I wonder if he thinks that.

"And we get to eat dessert first," Faith says. "And how come you know our Marley Bear?"

"We live near each other," Jack says.

"In the same house?!" Grace asks.

"Jack!" A kid is calling him from one of the benches. "What about that infield drill?"

Jack shrugs, which I think, I hope, means he wishes he didn't have to go.

"Let's get back," I say, flashing a smile of grown-up regret to Jack. "Let's go eat some junk."

"Cool," says Faith.

"Yeah, Marley," Grace says. "You're a cool bear."

"I'll see you later, Jack."

"Yeah, will me out."

* * *

I lead the twins back to the playground. They're peppering me with questions. "So whowazzat, Marley?"

"How come you know that guy, Marley?"

"Izzat your brother?"

"Jack is my friend. He lives near my dad's house."

"You got a mother, Marley Bear?" Grace asks, reaching for my hand.

"I do. She doesn't live with my dad, so I'm not staying with her right now. I live with her most of the time. A lot of the time."

"Your mother don't live with your father?"

"Right."

"Where does your brother live?" Faith asks.

"I don't have a brother. Or a sister. Just me."

"That's lucky," Faith says.

Grace looks sad, then mad.

"I don't think so," I say. "I think you guys are lucky to have each other. I'd love to have a sister."

Faith says, "Not lucky."

"We should find a place to wash your hands before we eat lunch."

"Eat dessert, you mean," Faith says.

"Well, both."

"Dessert first," Faith says. "You said."

"Clean hands first."

At once, both girls are spitting in their palms and then rubbing their hands together. They each rub their hands against their shorts and then hold them up. "Clean," Faith says.

"See?" Grace says.

"If it's good enough for you, it's good enough for me."

"I love Marley Bear," Grace says.

"Let's eat," I say.

The twins climb onto the bench by the fence and tear open the snack-size packs of cookies. "Kwee have drinks now?" they ask. I'm reaching into the cooler, opening drinks, then finding napkins to clean up the spilled drinks. The girls take off before they eat their sandwiches, back to the swings, where Faith swings high, standing on a swing, feet about a foot apart, like some tomboy version of Peter Pan. Grace practices her pumping. The swings squeak loudly, but I can still hear the metallic *ping* of a bat hitting a ball followed by the sounds of raised voices, cheering. Grace slows to a stop. When her swing is perfectly still, she climbs off and walks to the sandbox over in the corner. Faith joins her. I bring over my water bottle and a cup, and together we make a sand kingdom.

"I call I'm the nasty princess that knocks down stuff," Faith says.

"No, me!" Grace says. Not in a convincing way.

"And I'm the Marley Bear that gets angry at nasty princesses who knock down stuff. So let's not knock it over yet."

"When?"

"When you're *both* ready."

"I don't ever want to knock it down, Marley," Grace says.

"How about when Mommy gets here?" Faith asks.

Grace thinks about that. "Okay."

"You know any jokes, Marley?" Faith asks.

"Not a single one. I don't know any jokes."

"Marley Bear," Grace says. "Everyone knows jokes. I know that one about the black and white and red newspaper. It's not funny, maybe, but I know it."

"Okay. I know one."

"Go 'head," Faith says.

"Knock, knock."

"Who's there?" Grace says.

"Jonathan."

"Jonathan who?"

"Jon, a thin man just walked by."

"Marley?"

"Yes, Faith?"

"Isn't a joke opposed to be funny?

"I told you I didn't have any good jokes."

"I have one," Grace says.

"Go 'head," Faith says.

"Knock, knock."

"Who's there?"

"Tyler."

"Tyler who?"

"Tyler, a thin man just walked by." Grace starts to laugh, looks at me, then at Faith. "Not funny?" she asks.

Faith is about to say something mean when I begin to explain the Jonathan joke, and then rethink, realizing that a joke that requires explanation is probably not much of a joke at all. Also: they're five.

We concentrate on broadening our kingdom to the far reaches of the sandbox. When we hear Lynne's horn honk, I say, "One, two," and before I get to three, Faith is knocking it down. Grace is about to cry. I show her the turrets that are still standing, and she kicks them over. I gather together the picnic leftovers and containers and walk the twins to Lynne's car.

I help buckle them in and am about to climb into the passenger seat when Lynne says, "I have to take the girls with me now to Jenna's doctor appointment. Your dad said you could just walk home from here, that he'd meet you there. Is that okay?"

"Sure," I say.

"You gonna go and see your brother?" Faith says.

"I don't have a brother."

"Say goodbye to Marley, girls," Lynne says as she climbs back into the driver's seat.

"See you, Marley."

"Be a good bear," Grace says.

Comfortable and Familiar and Right

❧

I'm not sure if it's a dream or if it's just an image I get
in those strange minutes between being awake and
asleep, but whatever it is, it haunts me. It's the first day
of school. The halls aren't too crowded; I think the bell's
already rung. I'm walking down the hall. Leah and Jane
and some other kids are looking at me and whispering to
each other behind their hands. Someone is down at the
other end of the hall. As we get closer, we exchange
glances and nod, acknowledging each other, the way

members of the same species do. I turn and watch as the tan windbreaker disappears around the corner.

* * *

It sucks. It just sucks. How can I not have friends? How could my two best friends just let me fall out of their lives? Will I never hang out with Leah again? Jane? When I see them at school in September, will it be awful and awkward? Where's my life? This cannot be my life. All because I water balloon blitzed at the wrong time?

I cannot figure out how to steer off this course.

When it happens, it happens in the strangest way. Jack and I come back from walking Rig one Thursday afternoon and my dad's standing on the back porch, looking like he needs to tell me something.

"I saw Leah," he says. "Riding her bike."

"Really? Did you talk to her?"

"Yes, I did. She said she'd been trying to get in touch with you—texting, e-mailing—that she needs to talk to you. So I invited her over. She'll be here any minute."

"What are you talking about?" He must have misunderstood. Leah does talk really fast.

"I just thought . . ." His voice trails off and he seems to be staring very hard at me. I guess he didn't notice that I haven't seen Leah, or Jane, in weeks. It's not like I told him. He probably thought he was doing something really nice.

But wait. Leah's been texting me? And e-mailing me? Must find my phone. Must charge my phone.

"I figured we'd get in some pizza, you guys could play Monopoly, maybe watch a movie. Isn't that, I don't know, what girls do?"

I swallow a desire to stomp and scream that he needs to talk to me before he makes decisions for me. Through gritted teeth I ask, "Did she say when?"

Jack sort of backs away, calling, "See you soon, Marley."

I wave. And all of a sudden, throwing her bike on the lawn and racing toward me, there's Leah. "OH! My God, Marley! There you are!" she says, as though we hang out every day. Like she didn't just stop being my friend. She stands right in front of me and hugs me. *Hugs* me! "Is everything okay?"

No, Leah. I don't think everything is okay. But before my brain can even find words, she's off again, in pure Leah form.

"I mean, you don't answer texts or e-mails. I've left you like twenty voice mails. I've written on your wall, sent you messages on Facebook. *What* is going on?"

Seriously? "Why didn't you just . . ." But of course—Leah doesn't have my dad's new number. Why would she?

I explain about the stupid broken computer, and not charging my phone. But really, my brain's working at this as if it's a math problem written backwards in a foreign language. *Why is Leah here?* Did Jane turn on her too?

But the confusion is overtaken by something bigger and stronger—pure relief. I hug her back, about three minutes too late, and we both laugh at the stupid awkwardness. I pull her tight and think that whatever's behind us just needs to stay there, behind our backs. No turning around. No examining. Full speed ahead.

"So can you hang today?" Leah asks.

What about Jane? my mouth tries to ask, but I don't let it. "Definitely," I say. "What do you want to do?" The truth is, I don't care what we do. I'd go fishing with Leah right now if that was what she wanted. It's just so good to get back to normal, or learn this new kind of normal, normal without Jane. Which, I admit, doesn't feel at all normal. Yet.

We go inside, into my room. She sprawls on the bed and I sit on the floor, my back against the closet door. Everything I can think of to ask—*How's your summer?*

What's Curtain Call like? What have you been doing?—all comes way too close to Jane.

Leah must be bumping into the same thoughts herself, because there's this large silence in the room with us. I put on the radio and Leah finally comes up with "So what do you do for fun in this dump?"

"Absolutely nothing." What I want is to play Monopoly, I really do. It's always been something like my hands' version of comfort food. But after what Jane said, I don't think I'll ever speak the word *Monopoly* in front of Leah or Jane again.

Before we can sink into another deep pit of sucking silence, Leah has a brilliant stroke of conversational genius: she starts talking about wardrobe issues. And she's off.

She tells me about these two new pairs of shoes she got at the mall that I absolutely have to borrow, and somehow that leads to the story about this guy Karsten she liked in sixth grade, who just called her to see if she wanted to go to the movies. "'Yeah,' I told him, 'like, two years ago.'"

"You did not say that!"

"Well, not really. But I didn't go, either."

And it starts to feels right. Comfortable and familiar and right.

Leah-without-Jane has always been a slightly different person than the Leah of Leah-and-Jane-and-me. We never spent a ton of time together, just the two of us, but when we did, it was always good. So now it's just the two of us again. Maybe Jane-in-glasses is just a little too *all that* right now.

At some point after the pizza's delivered I realize my dad is nowhere to be seen. He must have been overwhelmed by all the girl vibes in the house. He and Rig probably snuck outside. I peek out the front window and see him catching a ball. I know it before I even look—there's Jack on the other side of the lawn, catching it and throwing it back. Jack? Is back? Already? Did he come here to will me outside? Did Dad intercept his message? Did Jack even mind or is it all the same to him?

It's no secret (except from Jack) that I've never been a huge baseball fan, but there is something about Jack's rhythm, the natural way he moves the ball from his gloved left hand into his right hand to throw, something about his long, thin legs, something loose and graceful that makes me want to stay by the window until it's too dark to see.

"Whatcha looking at?" Leah asks, her face suddenly next to mine.

I walk away. "Nothing," I say.

Leah keeps looking. "Mmm," she says. "Nice."

"You know," I say, needing to get Leah away from that window, from *mmm*ing Jack. "Cold pizza's disgusting. We should go finish it." I push her on her way and peek out the window one more time. Rig is fast asleep on his side beside the bushes, his legs moving—he must be having a chasing dream. Dad and Jack are talking, their profiles illuminated by the cast from the streetlight.

Why is Jack hanging out with my father? Is he just a lonely guy who spends time with anyone who'll have him? Maybe I shouldn't be so flattered that he seems to want to hang out with me.

I join Leah in the kitchen. "So do you want to watch a movie or something?"

"My mom has to pick me up soon," Leah says. "But let's do the movie soon."

Like tomorrow? I want to ask.

"Like tomorrow?" she asks.

Oh, I'm so glad she's back!

* * *

When she leaves, I find my phone charger and plug it in. And then Dad's house phone rings. He talks for a while, then calls for me to pick up.

"Hi, Marley. I miss you."

"Hi, Mom. I miss you too. How's Grandma?"

"She's great."

"I miss her."

"I know. She misses you. I miss you so much, too. Did your father say Leah's there?"

"She was. She just left."

"Jane too?"

"Uh, no." So much has happened and everything keeps changing. "So when's Grandma's surgery?"

"Later next week."

"She'll be glad to get that over with."

"It'll really make it so much easier for her to get around."

"Can I talk to her?"

"Sure—hold on."

There's a long pause, then the sound of the phone being pulled along a counter or something, and then I hear my grandma. "Hello there, Miss Marley Eden."

Only Grandma uses my middle name. "Hi, Grandma. Are you having a good summer?"

"It's nice to have your mom with me. I miss having you too."

"I know! I wish I were there."

"I do too. How's it going with your father?"

"Okay. I guess. Are you scared about the surgery at all?"

"Not so much," she says. "As I get older, the things that scared me don't look so menacing anymore."

"That must be nice."

"If you put a snake in my bed, I'd still scream."

"You know I'd never do that."

"I do. You're having a good summer, honey?"

I don't want to make her worry, but I don't lie to my grandmother. "There's a lot that's good," I say.

"I think that maybe that's the best you can hope for. I love you, Marley Eden girl. Your mom wants to talk to you again."

"So tomorrow you're back to the Land of Crazy Twins?" Mom asks.

"Yup. That's my summer."

"Is it any better?"

"I'm getting used to it."

"I'll give you a call soon. I love you. Be good. Listen to your dad, okay?"

"I'm not five."

"You're not. Bye."

My Normal Abnormal Way

First thing in the morning, I turn my phone on. It sounds like a hysterically broken doorbell, ringing for each of the messages I've gotten. They're all from Leah.

I start reading them, but it's all **Where r u** and **answer already!** and **call me!** Not the world's most entertaining reading. I'm deleting them when I get a new one: **Can i sleep over 2nite?**

I check with Dad and then text back yes.

* * *

Because this is the funnest summer ever, I get talked into helping my dad in the yard after babysitting.

But the lawn already looks so much better. There are almost no dandelions left.

"It looks great. Why don't we go out for ice cream instead?"

"Nice try, Marley. I mowed, but that's just temporary—gets rid of the flowers before they have a chance to go to seed. Now I need to eliminate the plants."

"You want me to dig out wherever I see the leaves?"

"That's my girl. No more talk of this dandelion recovery plan, this dandelions-are-flowers-too propaganda. Help me make this lawn a happy place where blades of grass can be free."

And so we work side by side, taking breaks for drinks. Well, one of us takes breaks.

He brings the radio outside, and the familiar sound of baseball talk carries on the summer air. I dig and pull and pile and pack it all into one of Dad's airtight, keep-the-bad-plants-away-from-the-good-plants containers, so there's no chance of reseeding. At one point he picks up a ball (where did that ball come from? Did Jack leave it here when he was playing catch with Dad?) and asks, "Feel like having a catch?"

I kind of want to, but I throw like a stotal paz. "I've

never learned the right way to throw, I don't think. Doctor, is it too late for me?"

"What kind of father didn't teach you how to throw? You throw fine. Let me see." And he tosses the ball to me gently.

I can't even throw my normal abnormal way because I'm thinking about it, trying to remember something about getting my elbow back. "I think thirteen might be too late to start," I say.

"I disagree. Here. Do this." And in slow motion, he pulls his arm back and goes through the throwing motion, stopping with his fingers wide open at the release point. "Ready?"

I try. I throw it as close as I can to the way he showed me, but I know I look lame. It reaches him, though. "How about you don't worry about form and we just throw the ball?"

"Okay," I say. I'm thinking it'll be about as much fun as fishing. It's a little better than that. I sort of feel like it's the least I can do for Dad, another small gesture. He seems so lost around me—the way he raced outside when Leah and I were hanging out—and this—balls, throwing—holds some kind of meaning for him.

So we stand and we throw. He throws grounders

and high pops, and we think up goofy challenges for each other, like under the leg while hopping. We throw until my arm starts to get sore.

"I think you should wrap my arm in ice and then a towel on top of that, and then I can walk around with one arm in my jacket sleeve. That would be cool."

"It would be." He smiles at me, a sad smile with a meaning I do not completely understand. "That was fun, Marley. Thank you."

"It *was* fun," I say, surprised that I'm not just telling him what I think he wants to hear. "When I come off the disabled list for overthrowing today, maybe we can do it again."

"Anytime."

* * *

We roll the TV and DVD player into my room. "So," Leah says. "Tell me what you've been doing all summer."

I tell her all about Grace and Faith and dandelion fairy princess crowns and how they snort and call me Marley Bear, and how nice Lynne seems. Even leaving out the part about playing catch with my daddy, as I'm talking, I realize how . . . young . . . my summer sounds compared to hers. She's acting, getting to know all these high school kids. I'm hanging with five-year-olds. Leah doesn't seem to notice. She can be a good listener when she finally stops talking. I let myself feel how much I've missed her, and the emotion is strong.

Later, when we're brushing our teeth before the movie, I decide to take a chance. I don't know where the courage comes from, and I don't take the time to debate whether it's courage or stupidity, but before it disappears, I blurt out, "Do you think Jane will ever speak to me again?"

"You really pissed her off. I mean, what could you have even been thinking?" She laughs, a laugh with an edge of something nasty. "She's seriously pissed."

"She was such a . . . I mean, the way she . . ." Leah was there. She saw. Why do I have to explain this? "It was awful, Leah. I made this horrible mistake, but it's not like I did it to be mean or hurt anyone. It was just stupid. But the way she yelled and hissed and screamed at me in front of everyone, it just—Ow. It just really hurt." I half expect the tiled floor to split like an earthquake movie set and for our bodies to slide right in. And I hate that I can't keep the tears from my eyes.

"She was really mad! I mean, no one should have to explain to you that when you're hanging out with high school kids, you don't play stupid little-kid games."

That awful, raw wound I felt the instant I stopped blitzing feels new again. And Leah's poking at it. Hard. With a filthy stick. I know what she's saying is true, but I can't undo it. All I can do is try to move on.

"I can try to talk to her for you, tell her you're really sorry and—"

"I'm not sure I want to keep apologizing."

"Come on, Marley. This is so stupid. Let me start to fix it. I'll tell Jane you're sorry and I'll get her to—"

"Do not tell her I'm sorry."

"Let me do this. I can do this for you."

This is all wrong. "I'm serious, Leah. Do not. Promise me."

"I don't get what the big deal is," Leah says. "I just want to fix—"

"I mean it, Leah. Promise me."

"Fine."

"You have to mean this. That you promise not to talk to Jane about me. Ever."

"I promise. Really. But maybe you should think about apologizing to her."

"But other than the balloon thing, which I totally admit was stupid, I didn't do anything wrong. And I already apologized for that. Or I tried to, and she was a scary alien witch. She hasn't exactly been the best friend to me either, you know."

Leah's eyes bulge, as if I've said the single most ridiculous thing that could ever be said. She does this thing with her hands, this sort of flicking away of something invisible. Something annoying.

"God, Marley. That is so you. Only seeing what you want to see. Think about it. You haven't exactly been a lot of fun since your parents split up." She leans over her small overnight bag, rifles through her stuff. "You're, like, depressed *all* the time. Trust me: *You* wouldn't even want to hang out with you. Maybe you should think about *that* before you tell me it's her and not you."

I want to scream, to accuse her and Jane of being the very worst kind of fair-weather friends, to shout that it's not at all true! To tell her that is an awful thing to say. But there's something about this feeling. I think I remember it. It's a raw-nerve feeling. Leah hit upon something true, something true that hurts.

That seems to be her special talent tonight.

I can scream all I want, but I can't make it untrue.

Have I really been so awful to be around?

I hear the front door close, and Rig and Dad step back into the house. Rig's trotting sound, nails on the hardwood floor, echoes as he goes through all the rooms, looking for me. When he finds me, it's as though we've been apart for months. He's so grateful I'm still here. I hold on to him.

Questions still hang in the air like low, swollen clouds. Did I just miss the signs for a long time? If I hadn't orchestrated the world's most awkward blitz, would there have been something else? Have Leah and Jane been trying to get rid of me? Does it even matter anymore?

And I don't like the way Leah's acting, as if I should be grateful for her willingness to help fix what's broken between Jane and me. Like she has all this power or something. It reminds me of Rig's *I could!* threat-jump at innocent bunnies. Like Leah's saying, *I could chomp you with my big giant dog teeth, Marley. I could make things better if I want to or I could make them worse. Make sure you know that, Marley.*

"Are you two going to start the movie now?" Dad calls in. "It's getting late."

I was hoping Leah would go home now. It might be healthy to talk things out, but I feel anything but healthy right now.

"Sure," I say.

And we watch, silently, until Leah falls asleep. Then I lie there, my body still but my mind buzzing, replaying this day. Not believing this day.

This Limbo

In the morning, Leah's still sleeping when I open my eyes. I grab some clothes from the top of the dresser and sneak into the bathroom to change so I don't wake her. Rig sits outside the door, and when I open it, dressed and ready, he thumps his tail in approval.

Outside, I try to look casual, but my eyes are like a sentry lookout's, scanning the horizon for signs of Jack. My whole body feels jazzed at the thought of just seeing him, of spending a few minutes talking to him, making up for the time we lost yesterday.

It's not like we had plans or anything, but I feel close to crying when I realize he's not out. I stare toward his house, my eyes locked on his back door with super willing-Jack-to-come-outside strength.

I must need some willing guidance. Rig comes over to me as though wondering why his friend isn't where he always is. Or maybe I inadvertently willed my dog over instead of Jack. He sits in front of me, then looks back in the direction of Jack's house. "I know," I say.

I sit down and start to pull dandelions out of the ground. This time, I decide to do it the right way. It's my dad's lawn. He may be claiming to be the new him, but I've been inside his closet. I've seen how he butters his toast.

It's never been easy for me to tell other people how I feel. It seems that even when I do, it's more work than it's worth. I felt like I was going to vomit last night with Leah, and what did that accomplish?

Since talking doesn't always work out for me, when I have an opportunity to show someone how I'm feeling, I try to take it. I guess it's the gesture language of the Baird family. Even though he can be a jerk, I miss my dad when he's not around, and I love him. I do. If he's overwhelmed by his life, well, I can sure relate. If he can't find the time to rid his lawn of dandelions, then I can help.

I don't know if he'll look at a pile of weeds pulled from the ground in the Robert Baird–approved method and know I'm trying to tell him that I love him. But I'll know.

I try to work without a tool, grasping hold near the root and pulling, but no matter how hard I pull, it leaves part of the root in the ground. I go to the garage and take out one of the many dandelion tools Dad bought before he settled on the one he sort of invented. This one's like a very long cookie cutter that reaches down low to get the whole scraggy root. Rig lies beside me as I work. Before long, the lawn around me is full of little holes, like some intense mini-golf course. I've never seen a lawn so infested before, and it's mind-blowing that I can pull out so many and hardly make a dent.

I hear a door slam shut and look toward Jack's house. It's a woman. His mom? She's wearing one of those short-sleeved pastel print smocks that the hygienists at my dentist's office wear. She puts what must be a cup of coffee on her car while she loads some things into the back seat. Then she takes a sip, looks back toward the house, climbs into the car, and pulls out into the street. Jack's mother works on the weekend?

I'm out for what feels like an hour before I hear Leah's voice. "Hey, Marley. Whatcha doing?"

Am I the only one who's quiet in the morning? "Just pulling out dandelions," I say, my voice a whisper.

"What are you doing today?"

"I'm not sure," I tell her. I have no idea what today will be like. I only know that I am smarting from the disappointment of not seeing Jack this morning. Also, how weird is it that I don't even want to talk about Jack with Leah? That's not quite it. I do want to talk about him with her, so much that I nearly start almost every minute, but part of me knows that it's not a good idea. That very thought is flashing in a corner of my brain like a giant warning sign. Also, Leah said some things that really hurt last night, and I want to crawl in a hole until I can start to figure it out.

"I've been thinking about what we talked about last night, Marley."

She's behind me and I'm looking down at the ground, at the holes left behind from digging down deep for all those far-reaching roots.

I want to say that we don't need to talk about it anymore because I'm sick of talking, and it doesn't make it better, and there's nothing she can say anyway.

"I'm sorry," she says.

"What kind of sorry?" I would have thought I'd be so thankful to hear her say those words. Instead, it unleashes some fury that has been growing, waiting. I am so mad at her and Jane for making me feel like I've lost my only friends in the world. For ditching me when I'm living through the hardest time of my life.

"For everything, Marley. It's just that Jane,—I don't know. When I'm with her, it all makes sense. When I'm with you, it all seems wrong. I am sorry. I'm sorry if we hurt you. I'm sorry I hurt you."

I must have been braced for her to say something lame. Because I feel something like a huge, rolling wave of relief soak me through to the edges. That was the exact right answer.

She walks over and hugs me. The tears that have been threatening every five minutes, anytime someone said something nice, come out in a hurry. I'm hugging her tight, and I'm sobbing, and I'm feeling so good. So grateful.

The front door opens and Dad is calling out for me. "Your mom is on the phone. Hey, are you okay?"

I'm drippy and snorffly, but I nod. "I'm good. I'll be right in."

Rig looks up at me, lying half on his back, and I know he's thinking that he doesn't want to go in right now, that the sun feels good on his side, that the grass feels right under his other side. "Just stay," I tell him.

When I get back outside, there's Rig in his sprawled-out-on-his-back position, with Jack rubbing his stomach in big, long ovals. Leah is standing right next to Jack. She takes two steps away from him when she sees me.

"Hey, Marley," Jack says.

"No camp today?"

"It's Saturday."

"Camp?" Leah asks. "You work at a camp?"

"No," Jack says, looking at the ground and toeing the dirt with his sneaker. "I just go to this baseball camp. I mean, I do sort of work there, but I also kind of go there."

I'm an idiot. Why did I have to bring up his camp and embarrass him? "So what are you doing?"

"Dean's supposed to pick me up. That's my brother," he says to Leah, leaning forward to look around the big maple and down the street. "I guess he's going to be late." He pulls a ball out of his pocket, tosses it up a little, and catches it.

"He doesn't live with you?" Leah asks, her eyes all earnest and interested and intent on Jack.

"No. He's older. He lives by himself."

"I have older sisters too!" she says, as if it is the

single most unbelievable coincidence of modern times. "One's away at college and one lives in Boston!"

Jack looks at her like he doesn't exactly get the connection. Then he looks back at me. "It's just a little weird, because we were supposed to get together today, but I haven't heard from him all week. Usually he calls. He'd better call." He takes the ball and hurls it hard against the maple tree.

"Oh, I hope he's okay," Leah says with a touch on his back.

Get your hands off him, Leah.

"If he doesn't show, maybe we could hang out," she says, her hand still casually on his back. "I mean, you should definitely hang with Marley and me. We could just hang, or walk Marley's dog, or whatever."

This is all too complicated. There's a war going on inside me. On one side—the soul-filling relief at being friends with Leah again, about being past the apologies and back to something normal. Or starting to build some new without-Jane normal. And on the other, the reality that Leah can sometimes be so annoying and flirty with the wrong people.

"Thanks," Jack says, "maybe I will, but I have a feeling he's going to show up this time. We're supposed to go up to the Bronx." He smiles at me. "To the game."

"They're playing the Orioles, right?" I feel like I need to prove something.

"Yup," Jack says. Then, with a smile, that eye-disappearing, dimple smile, he bends over and pats Rig's stomach, saying, "I'll see you later. I'm going to call him." He waves at both of us and sort of backs up a few steps before turning around and walking back to his house.

Leah has a smile on her face that I do not trust. I want to pelt her with water balloons. Or possibly stones. But I know her. If I said anything, she would act like I'm crazy. *Flirting? Trust me, Marley: I was so not flirting. You'd know when I was flirting.*

And I don't trust myself anymore. Is Leah doing anything wrong? Am I just jealous that I couldn't flirt even if flirting would save the lives of my immediate family? But Leah wouldn't flirt with Jack. This is just how she is; it was just Leah being Leah. I want to hug Leah and tell her I'm so glad we're friends again. I would also like to pull her hair and tell her never to look at Jack again.

I sigh and sit on the grass.

"What?" Leah asks.

"I'm not sure."

The sun's rays warm the top of my head with an

intense, no-joking heat. Summer heat. The hot air feels full of the essence of cut grass, exactly the way it's smelled every summer for the past thirteen years. Everything's the same, and everything's different.

I hate not knowing. If I knew Leah and I had worked everything out and it was all cool for us from now on, I could live with having felt like the left-out loser for a little while. Or if I knew that my parents ended up back together—that would have to be easier than this limbo. Not knowing feels worse than anything.

And I wish I knew if Jack and I would become friends beyond just this summer. Or maybe even more than friends. That one's a little different, though, because at the same time, this, the finding out, is amazing. I'm savoring the delicious excitement of not knowing how it works out, the hopeful suspense of living through each tiny new experience that creates what exists between Jack and me. As my dad says when the Yankees play loser teams, you never know how it'll turn out. That's why you have to play the game.

Ace of the Earth

Leah and I make breakfast for my dad—pancakes, pulpy orange juice, and a few strips of bacon. We make up some big heaping plates for ourselves too. I pour my orange juice through a strainer I find under the stove to remove all the pulp.

Working with Leah in the kitchen, reaching over her for the baking powder, around her for the flour, I'm aware of how it feels, as if we've almost clicked into place again. But it also feels like there's a shadow of unease lurking at the corners, darkening, seeping.

"What do you two have planned for today?"

Leah shrugs. "Just hanging, I think."

"Actually," I say, "I might try to get to the library. I have to check my e-mail, since I can't do that here." I pause for a minute, letting that sink in with him. "And I want to get some books to read to the twins."

"I don't know if you have plans tonight, Leah, but you're welcome to stay here with Marley. I'll be going out for a little while, and—"

"Where are *you* going, Dad?"

"I'm meeting a friend for dinner."

"What friend?" The people he and Mom go out with are all couples. Have they divvied up their friends? Do they take turns?

"Lynne." If I'm not mistaken, my very own father is blushing.

Leah snorts. Just like a twin.

"Lynne who?"

"Lynne Kroll."

"Kroll like the Krolls, like the twins?"

He nods. His face is still bright red.

"Is Mr. Kroll meeting you for dinner too?"

"Mr. Kroll isn't living with his family. You haven't noticed that, Marley?"

"I'm there when most normal people are working, right?"

"Well, I suppose that's true," he says, focusing an unusual amount of concentration on using his fork to cut the remaining small piece of pancake into smaller, equal-size pieces. "I thought it might be obvious that there's not a male presence in that house."

"But they just had a baby."

"He actually left before Jenna was even born. He's only seen the baby once."

Leah looks like a wide-mouthed frog. I could shove four hot dogs in her open mouth. I know what she means—this is way too much info for one breakfast conversation—but she should shut her mouth.

So the twins' father is not there. And my dad is . . . Oh, gross. But is he meeting her for dinner, maybe, to just talk about me and how it's working out? Then why would his face have burned so red? Ew. It's not enough he has to play ball with Jack? He has to have dinner with Lynne too?

"It's just dinner, Marley. I don't want you freaking out about this."

I am so not freaking out about this. Why does he think I'm freaking out about this? "How'd you even meet her?"

"At a meeting. At the library once a month there's a meeting for people going through divorce. We met there."

Going through divorce. Like beyond being separated. Moving ahead, going through with it. Maybe there are no meetings for parents who are just separated. Maybe it's just the closest fit.

"Well, this was delicious, ladies. I thank you." He stands and takes his dish and silverware from the table to the sink. "And now, Marley, you may be saddened to learn that I am off once again to seek and destroy dandelions. I'm going win the Battle of the Lawn at last." He walks out the back door. I wonder, briefly, if he'll notice the dandelions I've pulled, and how I got all the roots.

"OH! My God," Leah says. "Do not tell me it is Saturday. Just do not."

"Really? 'Cause it is."

"Just kill me. I hate to say this, but I have to get out of here! I was supposed to do a read-through with . . . OH! My God. I'm so dead. I'm sorry to skip out on you, Marley. I—"

"Just go. It's fine."

"No. I want to hang with you more. We have to catch up. Can I come back later?"

"Yeah, sure."

She calls her mother to pick her up and packs her things while I clean up in the kitchen. I'm wiping down the counter when I hear the honk of her mother's black Explorer. The three of us used to call it Dora, and we thought that was the funniest thing anyone had ever thought of.

"I'm gonna go now," she says. "Wish me luck on the read-through! I'm reading with this hottie, Ethan."

Ethan. Callie's boyfriend. "I hope everything works out."

"It always does." Leah laughs as she walks out the door. "See ya."

I watch them pull out of the driveway, past Dad's cartons, still stacked at the curb. There really must be some new-him in my dad, as the Dad I used to know would have been on the phone with the town every day, demanding that his trash be picked up at once.

I step outside. My dad is standing on the front lawn in his gardening clothes, pouring something that might be vinegar, judging from the stench, over the low stems of each dandelion plant.

"Do you feel like a murderer?" I ask him, stepping off the porch and onto the lawn.

"Only in the best way," he says. "Freeing the individual blades of grass from the tyranny of unwanted intruders."

"That's what all evil rulers say." I sit on the lawn and then stand when I feel the wet soak through my shorts.

"Did you have fun with Leah?" Dad asks.

"Not exactly fun," I say.

"Do you want to talk about it?"

"Want to? Not exactly."

"Do you not exactly want to help me too?" He holds out his dandelion elimination tool with a hopeful look.

"Again?" I ask.

"Yes. Again."

"Maybe once I get back from the library?"

He nods.

"I'd totally do it now, of course, if I didn't have to go to the library to use a computer, but my dad's computer? It's still broken? And he didn't pay for an Internet connection? So I haven't been able to go online all summer? And—"

"Goodbye, Marley."

I grab an old backpack for books and set off on my bike.

* * *

There's a wait for computer time, of course, so I put my name on the list at the head librarian's desk.

In the DVD aisles, I pull a few out but put them back when I realize there's no way I'm going to be done with them in two days. Two-day DVD loans, library? Really?

I'm heading into the kid and teen room—a hilarious mix of baby ducks and kittens on one wall and vampires on another. I'm stepping aside into the bathroom entranceway to let three people pass, when I realize one of them is Jane's sister Sammi. I look up. Sammi and her mother. And, with her head not looking up from texting, Jane.

"Marley!" Sammi says, hugging me. "I haven't seen you! I miss you!"

"How are you, Marley?" her mother asks. "Jane, stop that. Say hello."

Jane does not stop texting.

Jane does not look up.

Jane does not say hello.

Jane-in-glasses keeps looking down, fingers working the tiny keyboard furiously.

"Jane!" her mother says.

Jane looks up. She slowly tucks her hair behind her ear. She says, "Eh." Or maybe "Uh." Or possibly "Oh."

And then she walks away.

"Did you ever read this, Marley?" Sammi asks.

Grateful to have something to do other than melt into the gross library carpet, I look at the book she's holding. It has a dog and a potbellied pig on the cover. I smile. "I have. It's funny."

Sammi hugs the book to her stomach.

Jane's mother looks mortified.

"Well, bye," I say, turning around and walking back to the adult section as quickly as I can.

"Send your parents my best," Jane's mother calls.

I turn and see two people step away from computer desks, so I check and yes, it's my turn.

It would be best not to think now. Not to think about how awful that was. And definitely not to think about how what just happened will translate into my daily life in school. Not to picture the same thing playing out in the hallways over and over and over.

I get online. Finally.

E-mail first. A lot of old stuff from Leah, from before she knew I was computerless. Forwarded jokes from Uncle Stu, Dad's brother. I hate forwarded jokes but save that message to see if there's anything Grace and Faith might like. An e-mail from my cousin in Chicago.

And that is all.

Wow.

Nothing doing on Facebook.

Nothing happening anywhere.

I haven't been missing anything.

And no one has been missing me.

*   *   *

I ride my bike home, my body feeling the same super-charged way it did the one time I watched a horror movie.

I have never seen a dead person. But I've read that even if someone just died seconds earlier, they don't look asleep; you can tell that they're dead. Something is gone.

That's exactly how it felt with Jane. There was nothing there. Nothing. My brain has a hard time getting it—we were best friends forever, but now there's nothing. The word *chilling* keeps going through my mind. It's chilling.

At home, I put my bike in the garage and text Leah:
When will u be here?

She doesn't answer. I spend the rest of the afternoon listening to the game with my dad, weed whacking around the bushes, and pulling crabgrass out of the backyard flower garden. When balls at the game are hit foul, I think of Jack and wonder if any are landing near where he's sitting.

"Marley," Dad says as he's gathering up cut-down weeds in his garden-gloved hands. "Tell me why you didn't have a good time with Leah."

I do my own version of his air cough of annoyance.

"And why haven't I been seeing Jane around? Is something going on?"

"I'm not exactly talking to Jane," I say. I get an actual chill down my back when I think about the way she walked right past me in the library, as if I wasn't even there. And then I feel a sickening wave of shame when I realize it's probably not that different from how I always passed poor Elsie Jenkins in her tan windbreaker.

"I don't want to talk about this right now."

"Did I ever tell you about Lou Gehrig and Babe Ruth?"

"I'm sure you did," I say. "I wasn't listening."

"Here, take this," he says, handing me a giant trash bag. "Make sure you get all the weeds on that side," he says. "Anyway, they had some little fight over something that really didn't matter, and they didn't talk to each other for six years. Years during which they were team-mates, together all the time. They didn't talk until Lou Gehrig Appreciation Day."

I nod my head the whole time he talks—another baseball story. "Yeah, yeah, yeah," I say. "When Gehrig gave that echoing speech. I consider myself, -ider my-self . . . the luckiest man, -uckiest man . . . on the face of the earth, -ace of the earth." I've heard this part of the story thousands of times. Lou Gehrig was already sick then. He died a couple of years after that.

"I've always wondered if the Babe and Lou regret-ted letting that misunderstanding keep them from talk-ing all that time. Six years thrown away, just being mad at each other. That's a waste. Maybe you can work it out," Dad says.

What a Dad thing, a teacher thing. Tell a little story, a fable, a cautionary tale and guide the way to fix a problem.

"It's not that simple," I say. I try to picture Lou Gehrig unleashing water balloons in a surprise blitz or Babe Ruth rudely ignoring Lou in the back hallways of Yankee Stadium, but the image shifts and baseballs are flying out of a bathroom window and into a stadium, and then Jack's there too. (*What? That's the nature of daydreams and fantasies. They get weird.*) Luckily my father stops talking.

We're listening to the postgame report (because a half-hour pregame and three-hour ball game isn't enough baseball for me! I need to hear it all summarized and analyzed!) when Dad and I finally finish up. "We don't need to bother watering," he says. "Mother Nature will take care of that." I look up and see that the sky is clouding over. He goes into the house.

I text Leah again: When r u coming over?

Why isn't she answering?

Why do I always assume that when she's not with me, she's with Jane?

And why do I feel nearly certain that the only reason Leah spent time with me this weekend was because Jane was too busy for her?

The wind starts blowing hard. Rig and I head inside. I sit on the couch with the newspaper and flip to the entertainment section. I think about seeing a movie later, but who, exactly, would go with me?

Are dogs allowed in theaters?

The wind is really starting to howl now; thin-trunked trees bend like dancers warming up.

Dad's getting-ready noises carry to the living room.

I turn on the TV and put the volume up high. I can picture him arranging what he's going to wear. Getting dressed, taking the neat roll of bills and short stack of change from his dresser and placing them in his right front pants pocket. I don't want to witness my dad leaving on his first date since moving out. Is it even a date? I don't want to think about it. I yell into his room, "I'm going outside."

"Isn't it raining?" he asks.

Now it's actually starting to brighten a bit—one of those storms that threatens and then backs off. "I think it blew over. I'll see ya."

Before I get out, he says, "I'll leave you money for dinner, if you want to get something delivered."

"Have a good night."

"Thanks, Marley. I won't be late."

There is something repulsive about that. Shouldn't I be saying that to him?

Just Trying to Move On

B efore the door has even closed behind me, I can see that there's something all over the lawn. It takes me a few seconds to understand what it is, and then a few more to realize how it got there. The wind from the storm-that-wasn't must have tipped over one of the trash cartons out at the curb. The contents of the old Monopoly box have been blown everywhere. There are yellow hundred-dollar bills in the rosebush. Title deed cards line the curb, some turned upside down, the way you flip them when you have to mortgage the property.

I walk around the yard, looking for the box. Some bills are blown a few houses down the street. Treasure Chest cards are clumped together under a tree near the curb. The Monopoly board and the game's three remaining pieces—the hat, the dog, and the shoe—are still in the bottom of the box, which only blew into the gutter, but almost everything else is all over the place.

I put the box back on the pile of cartons and go inside to grab a garbage bag from under the kitchen sink. When I head back out to gather up the pieces, I hear Jack right away: "Did you will me out to help you?"

"How could you be back already? Did you fly home?"

"My brother wanted to leave early to beat the traffic. It sucked. We were out of the stadium in the bottom of the sixth."

"Oh, that does suck."

"When I drive, I will never leave a game early." He looks at me. "So, did you will me out?"

"I didn't think you were home, so no." Not unless you count this morning. Maybe my message was delayed. "But I could use some help."

He starts to pick up the game pieces. "What happened here?"

I bite my lower lip. "Tragic Monopoly accident." I

hope for a laugh. I get a smile and a handful of white one-dollar bills. "The wind must have knocked over some of these boxes," I say, tilting my head toward the street, where the stacks of cartons are starting to look a little nasty. "Don't they ever pick up trash around here?"

He shrugs. "There are some weird rules about bulk trash, I think."

"Did you have a good time at least?"

"Pitchers' duel," he says.

"I know. I was listening."

We work side by side, gathering and shoving things in the trash bag.

"You know what we should do?"

"Put my dad's cartons in bags so this doesn't happen again?"

"Close. We should go to a Yankees game together. That would be so cool. Dean was saying he wasn't sure he could go to the next game we have tickets for, so why don't you come with me? It's on . . . I can't remember the date. The first Sunday of August. Do you think you can go?"

"I'll ask. Can I let you know?"

"Definitely."

Before I can even start to feel excited or maybe nauseous about the very idea of Jack and me at a game to-gether, just the two of us, he says, "So how was today?"

"All right."

"Your friend seems cool."

It's unlikely that he really kicked me in the stomach with a steel-tipped shoe, but it feels like he did. Why? I don't want him hating my friends. Of course, I don't exactly want him loving my friends either. "It's compli-cated, I guess. The things we used to do together don't seem like much fun anymore."

"Like what?"

"Like playing Monopoly."

"So you just threw out the game? Harsh." He hands me some cards and says, "Park Place, Saint James, Elec-tric Company."

I think to myself: *Park Place/straighten opponents' money piles; Saint James/do ten jumping jacks; Electric Company/cross eyes and squawk.*

"Thanks," I say, taking the cards from his hand and putting them in the trash. "This was just an old one; we threw it out before Leah even came over. I have a new one."

"I've always liked Monopoly," Jack says as he reaches behind a crepe myrtle bush for a stack of pink five-dollar bills.

"Yeah, me too. The three of us—me and Leah and Jane—used to play this weird way, like it was almost a whole different game."

"Yeah? How'd you play?"

"Long story," I say. "And ancient history. I think."

"Who were you?"

"Marley Baird. Nice to meet you. I still am, by the way. Who might you be?"

"Funny. No, I mean which piece are you?"

"Guess."

"Dog."

"Right. Always. You too?"

"Actually, I'm a racecar kind of guy."

"Leah's always been the hat. Jane was the shoe."

The weight of how all that is in the past now feels like a superstrong gravity, pulling me down. Jack must feel it too, because neither of us can think of a thing to say. "Can I tell you something?" I say, flailing around inside my head, not yet sure which of the many percolating thoughts is going to come out, just desperate to pull us out of the brutal quicksand of social awkwardness we're sinking in.

He shrugs.

"My dad is like going out with the woman whose twins I've been babysitting. That's where he is right now—out to dinner with her. I mean, I know he and my mom aren't together, but they're not exactly divorced either, just separated, and it's just really creeping me out."

He doesn't respond at first. "So wait a minute," he finally says. "Do you mean you're babysitting for your dad's girlfriend's kids?"

"Oh, I . . . Huh." Why did I assume this was the first time they were going out? Maybe because my father isn't the biggest jerk, the most manipulative parent alive. And he'd have to be to volunteer his daughter to babysit for his new girlfriend's kids. I stand, tie the Monopoly trash bag up, and walk it to the trash can. "I don't know what to do," I say. I sit on the curb, my feet in the street. Jack sits next to me.

"About what?"

"Everything," I say. It feels like an understatement.

Rig walks over to Jack. He sits next to him and wags his tail expectantly. "Ruh," he says.

"Does he want to walk or something?"

"I think he willed you to say that," I say.

"Do you want to?"

"Leah said she was coming over, but I haven't heard from her, so sure," I say.

We head to the park. The night is getting dark, but

the air feels light. The storm-that-wasn't seems to have taken all the humidity with it. The woods on the path are lit up with fireflies, and Rig looks like a stotal paz, chasing them without any success. Jack and I keep laughing at him, all the way to the park and across the soccer fields. And there, in the playground, are Faith and Grace. How's that possible, if their mother is . . . But there's Lynne, and there's my dad, pushing Jenna in a carriage. Okay. Sure. Yeah, of course.

Rig runs over before I can turn and run home or hide behind a tree. "Hey! Marley! Jack!" Dad calls, sounding genuinely happy to see us.

"I thought you were going out to dinner," I say. My voice sounds dead.

"Actually," Lynne says, "just dinner at my house. We were trying to tire out the girls so they'd sleep." Why do they need the girls to sleep? I wonder if she cleaned the kitchen. I wonder what he'll think of that chaotic house. Or has he been in there many times before?

My body is struck from two sides.

"Marley Bear!"

"Marley Bear!" Grace wraps her arms around my right leg, and Faith has her arms around my waist. They start jumping up and down while still holding me, like a team greeting the game-winning batter at home plate.

"Hey, you two," I say. "Do you remember my friend Jack?"

"Hi, Jack," Faith says.

Grace peers around my leg to look at him and smile.

"I've been hearing a lot about you," Jack says.

"Really? What did you hear about us?"

"Did you two see my dog?" I ask, trying to pull Faith away from Jack. "This is Rig. Come say hi."

"What did Marley say about us to you?" Faith wants to know.

I will not be able to walk home. Ever. I'm going to need an airlift. An ambulance. Or a bunch of kindly woodland creatures. My dad and Lynne together is just too weird. And way, way too much.

"Have you guys caught any fireflies tonight?" I ask as I try to twist my body gently from Grace's grip.

"I don't like flies," Grace says. "They're gross."

"All kids like fireflies. They're magic, like . . . I don't know. Tinkerbell."

And Rig's off again, doing his absurd fly-chasing dance, chomping at the air as he tries to catch one.

"Something's wrong with your dog, Marley," Grace says.

My dad leans in and says, "He's been trying to catch

a fly for six years now. That's what he looks like when he's chasing a fly."

"Six years?" Faith asks. "How hard could it be?" And then she's off, following the quick yellow lights that pulse in the early night sky.

"I'll help you," Jack says, following her.

My dad sits on a bench and rocks Jenna's carriage back and forth. Lynne sits next to him. Ugh. Why did I look?

"I caught one!" Faith yells.

"I wanna catch one!" Grace says. "What do I do with it once I catch it?"

Just then, in front of all of us, Rig opens his mouth and clear as day in the darkening night, a firefly goes right in. Rig sits, closes his mouth. It twitches, looks like it wants to open, but he's keeping it shut. His tail thump, thump, thumps the ground, as though he's saying, *I did it!*

"Marley!" Grace screams. "MAR-LEY! Your dog ate Tinkerbell!"

"Make him stop," Faith says. "Why'd your dog do that, Marley?"

Then Rig lets out this weird yelp, almost like he's been stung, and when he opens his mouth, the bug flies out. It heads toward the monkey bars, and the girls race behind it.

"Come here, Rig." I kneel in front of him and open his mouth. Could firefly light be dangerous for dogs? Rig stands up and shakes.

"We should probably go back and get him some water," I say. "Hey, Grace! Faith! I'll see you Monday, okay?"

"Bye, Marley Bear!" they yell out together.

"Bye, Dad. See you, Lynne."

I reach deep inside my spent energy bank to find the strength to walk very quickly away from all that. Jack lags, waving goodbye to the girls.

"Ugh," I say when he finally catches up to me. "You were right."

"About what?"

"She *is* his girlfriend."

"Well, don't laugh, but now I'm thinking maybe I was wrong. I mean, you don't really know—"

"Huh? Hello? She makes him dinner and he pushes her baby around and ugh, I'm going to be sick. Did you see him pushing that baby? I really think I'm going to throw up."

"Well, yeah—"

"So how come you're on his side?"

"I'm not, Marley. I just think you might be jumping to conclusions."

I stop walking and face him. He looks ridiculously sure of himself. "It's bad enough he's hooked up with some stupid girlfriend, but getting me to watch her kids?"

His hands are in his shorts pockets, and he shrugs as if this is no big deal at all. "I get why this is weirding you out, but they really could just be friends. It *is* possible."

I get an image of a high-flying ball soaring from Dad's glove, up in the air—way over my head—to Jack's glove, and back again, in an endless arc, far out of my reach.

We start walking again, dry pine needles crunching underfoot. In a quiet voice Jack says, "Have you ever thought, maybe your father's just trying to move on?"

"He's still married to my mother, or doesn't that even matter?"

"So is that it? You think they might get back together?"

I don't think hoping for something is the same as thinking it. I also don't think it's any of his business right now.

"I'm just not exactly thrilled that my father left my mom and me, and now I'm babysitting for his stupid girlfriend's kids. Can't you get that?"

"I think your dad's a good guy," he says. "I guess I'm trying to see it from his point of view."

"You know what, Jack? You just go ahead and do that."

"What are you so pissed about?"

"You."

He stops walking again. He looks ready to shut down. Shut me out. Good. Who cares? What else do I have to lose?

"It seems like you want to be mad at him. Or mad at someone."

"Like you know so much about me!"

"Maybe I don't."

"Ya think?" He might be cute, but I think he might also be a total jerk. It's too much. I can't stand it anymore. I feel like I got on the kind of ride I'd never go on, the kind of nightmare I have all the time. It's way too scary and twisty and upside down. All I ever wanted was to stay on the kiddie boats that go in gentle little circles in shallow water. I'm holding on, just trying to believe that I'll be all right, that it will end. That everything will be all right.

"So, good *night,*" I say, disgusted with Jack and all his opinions.

I walk home.

Alone.

Dandelion Wishes

I avoid my dad all day Sunday—read, sleep, walk dog, repeat. But there's no more hiding when we're back to Monday, in the truck on the way to Grace and Faith's. I can't quite look at my dad, or even start a normal conversation with him. "I don't want to know one thing about Saturday night, so don't talk to me about Saturday night."

"Right," he says. "Are you okay?"

"Sure."

"Are you ready for a day of twins?"

"I guess." We may as well be fishing.

The girls are waiting for me outside. Grace is wearing a sleeveless Tinkerbell shirt with Minnie Mouse shorts and Faith has on an oversize man's shirt with a picture of a can of beer. They're both gripping big bundles of dandelions in their hands. It's a total mix, from bright yellow flowers to giant puffballs.

"For you, Marley."

"I missed you," Grace says as she hands me her bouquet.

"Okay, each of you take one of these." I hand them each a puffball. None of them is a perfect globe anymore, as they've been handled too much by five-year-old hands and some of the seeds have already fallen off. But they're good enough. "This kind of dandelion, this puffball, is a magic ball. When you blow it, its powers are released."

"I blown 'em before. But I didn't know about powers. What powers?" Grace asks.

"Special magic powers."

"Like fairy powers?" Faith wants to know.

"Kind of. Make a wish," I say.

"Like a balloon wish?" Grace asks. "Like when you let go of a balloon?"

"Do I have to tell you my wish?" Faith asks.

"Yes, Grace. No, Faith."

"Can I tell you my wish?" Grace asks.

"I think it's supposed to be secret."

Grace nods slowly, seriously.

"So what you do is close your eyes and make your wish, and then you try to blow all the seeds off the dandelion with one breath."

"I can do that!" Faith starts puffing at the dandelion, and when all the seeds don't fall off at once, she starts shaking as she blows, until the stem is bare. Grace does the same.

"Excellent job," I say.

"Marley?"

"Yes?"

"Are wishes real?" Grace is gazing at my face, just waiting for the answer she wants. I have a feeling her wish was about her father, and it just kills me to think I may have planted a false hope by telling her there was magic. What if she spends the rest of the day, the rest of the summer, looking at the driveway, waiting for her father to pull up with a pile of packed suitcases and a heart full of past regret and better intentions for the future? I know better than to be promising happy endings to these two.

But they're five. Just about the only benefit of being five is still believing your wishes can come true. "I think wishes are real," I say. "I don't know if they always come true—I don't think they do. But the wish is definitely still real."

She looks at me for a while, maybe trying to understand, maybe thinking I'm from Mars. "I think what you should do is put a dandelion in a balloon and float it to the sky. That's like two wishes then. And maybe even pray when you're doing it too, so it's like three."

I have worked very hard to banish all thoughts of balloons since the Fourth, but there's something about that image that really appeals to me. A dandelion somehow suspended inside a balloon, slowly rising away from the earth.

"I'm getting more dandelions! I want more wishes!" Faith takes off toward the back of the yard, near the hill where the bunnies race.

"Wait for me!" Grace screams. "Leave some for me!"

As I watch them, I try to imagine what it would have been like for me if my dad had moved out eight years ago. How do their little five-year-old hearts hold all that sadness? Would I have been nicer to them all summer if I knew that they were dealing with the same hard stuff as me?

As they run back toward me, blowing, eyes closed, I try to figure out what they might need, what might help them. My parents, in their different ways, would try to get them to talk about it. Leah and Jane would have done the opposite—tried to change the subject whenever they talked about it. I don't know what's right, so I just promise myself to try to be nicer to them.

I hear the screen door slap shut. "Open your eyes when you're running!" Lynne screams from the porch. I wince, realizing I should have said that. Then I'm thinking, hmm, she's comfortable leaving me, inexperienced, unlicensed me, alone with her kids for weeks and she saunters outside when it's convenient to judge how I watch them? She turns to me and asks, "They're making dandelion wishes?"

What's this? Some veiled criticism about me letting her kids spread dandelion seeds all over their lawn? It's a mess anyway. Just because she might be my dad's girlfriend doesn't mean I can just entertain her kids all day and keep them from blowing dandelion seeds and making her lawn worse.

Did I really once think she was nice?

She looks like she's waiting for an answer. "Yeah, they're just making wishes," I say. "Dandelions never lasted long enough on my lawn for me to make wishes. My dad's like a lawn nazi." Is she going to tell my father everything I say?

"What'd you say, Marley Bear?" Grace asks, pulling at a belt loop on my shorts.

"I never got to blow dandelions at my house when I was your age."

"How come?" Grace is practically climbing me, trying to wrap herself around my leg.

"My father's sort of a dandelion hater."

"That doesn't surprise me," Lynne says.

Yeah, because you know him so well.

"No bunnies for Marley," Faith says. "No dandelions for Marley."

"Poor Marley!" Grace hugs my leg and pats my lower back. "Is your mother mean too?"

I laugh. "No. She's not mean." She's just away. And not that good at returning phone calls.

"It really wasn't too bad," I tell the girls. "My grandmother always let me blow dandelions all over her yard. I made ton of wishes." I think about those wishes now, and they seem so simple—a red bike, a trip to Disney World. I should have made just one, a big one:

Please, oh please, let things stay exactly as they are now.

"We had a lot of different theories about dandelions when I grew up," Lynne says. Was her voice always this annoying? "My Aunt Bemmy always said that if you rubbed the fluid from inside the stem of a dandelion on a wart, it would make it go away."

"Hmm," I say. The twins set off again, scouring the lawn. Grace runs alongside Faith until Faith trips her and takes the lead.

Grace looks around, as though she's deciding whether or not to cry, then gets up and follows her sister.

"There was another dandelion trick where I grew up," Lynne says. "Take one of the yellow flowers, Marley."

Why is she out here today? Shouldn't she be holed up in her little office? Who's watching Jenna? I put the other flowers down and hold a perfect yellow dandelion.

"Now hold it under your chin," she says.

I do. She starts to look at my neck, from left to right, then back again, concentrating on something, looking at me so closely that I can't look back. I look down, but all I see is the flower.

"They say that you can tell if the person holding

the flower is in love from the reflection of yellow on her neck."

I don't know if my neck is yellow, but I do know, without even being able to see it, that my face is bright red. Does she get off on embarrassing people? Stealing fathers away from Perfectly Good Lives and having dinner with them?

And I'm not in love with Jack anyway. Obviously. Stupid know-it-all Jack. I'm disgusted with him.

"We used to eat them too." Will she ever shut up? "We'd make salads, fritters, even ice cream."

"How 'bout that?"

Faith and Grace keep running back to pile more dandelions (and other things that are not dandelions) on top of the bunches they already handed me.

Lynne is still droning on. "And my mother—she grew up in England—she said people there believed that if you smelled a dandelion, you'd wet your pants."

The twins start to scream with laughter. I have never heard children laugh so hard. Grace falls down and Faith falls on top of her.

"I'm going to get back to work now," Lynne says. "You seem to have things under control out here."

That she could look at a pile of laughing, snorting twins and consider that under control worries me. Was she checking on me, making sure I was working? What happens here when I'm not around?

Faith and Grace both try to stand up and then fall right back down, howling with laughter, gasping for breath. Before long, they regain what passes for their composure. Then Faith stands and walks over to the pile of dandelions she picked earlier. "Marley Bear?" she says.

I know what's coming. "Yes, Faith."

"I need you to smell this dandelion."

"I don't think I can help you with that."

Grace stands up and approaches me from the other side.

"You're going to have to, Marley."

"Why's that?"

"'Cause we wanna see if it's true."

"You smell it," I say.

"No! You! YOU!"

"You. Are. Angering. The. Marley. BEAR!"

They scream again and take off in different directions, like fireworks snaking down to the ground. I hear one of them, not sure which, start to taunt "Marley's scared of peeing!" I'm pretty sure it's Faith. It always is.

* * *

When I'm ready to leave, Lynne steps onto the porch. "Can I speak with you for a minute, Marley?"

Can I say no?

"Are you okay?" she asks.

"Fine."

"Is something wrong?"

Please don't, lady. I might break. I don't answer, my eyes locked on the gray porch floor.

"Anyway, I just wanted to thank you, Marley. The girls are really enjoying their time with you." I'll bet she's only saying this because she knows kindness makes me cry.

I fight to keep myself from squirming. I have to say something. "I was wondering," I say. "Could we go to the park again one of these days, maybe with their bikes? I think they'd really like that."

There's something in Lynne's eyes—maybe memories about when she was there with her husband, when the twins were babies? "Sure, whatever you'd like. I'm sure they'd love that."

"Thanks."

"Thank *you*, Marley, for everything."

What a bitch; she's being nice.

In a House Atop the Trees

⌒

It's gotten so bad that some days, most days, my time at the Krolls' is the high point. I've lost one of my best friends. And now even Leah's being weird. She stood me up and now she doesn't answer her texts or voice mails. It's not that different from how it was before we started to work everything out; I'm still alone.

But the worst part is that everything is all screwed up with Jack. I've been avoiding him since he became my dad's top defender. His number one fan.

And I can't help wondering if *I'm* the problem.

Maybe whatever it was that drove Jane away is having the same repelling effect on Jack. Now that he's seen the angry and depressed me, the real me, there's no spark of anything special between us anymore. We sometimes say a quick hello in the mornings, when I'm out with Rig, but he hasn't been willing me out after work and I haven't gone looking for him. I keep thinking he'll come over to remind me about that Yankees game we're supposed to go to, or say something, anything to make it better, but he doesn't. And I can't figure out a way to do it myself.

The only person who ever calls me is my mom. She talks about her new old friends and getting Grandma ready for surgery. Sadly, these conversations are often the most exciting of my day.

I'm a total no-friends loser who almost looks forward to spending time with five-year-olds because at least, for minutes at a time, it takes my mind off everything else. Except that the twins' mother is there too and I get a very uneasy feeling whenever I'm near her.

And then, of course, things get even worse during a game of tag. Grace and Faith are running in frantic circles in the backyard, and I can't even remember who's "it," but it doesn't matter because they're both laughing and running like scary wild things, and then, out of no-where, I hear a howl. A loud scream of a howl. Grace is on the ground—she's cut her leg, pretty badly, on the old metal table, and she's bleeding.

I help her to her feet and hold on to her while she hobbles in the back door. Faith goes to get their mother. Lynne gets weird—sort of frantic, yelling. "I have to call the pediatrician. Or Ed. Someone!" She opens drawers, lifts out papers, and slams the drawers shut again.

I want to say, *It's just a cut,* but she is in full frenzy.

"I have no idea where Ed filed their immunization forms, and if Grace isn't up to date on tetanus, well then, we have a really big problem here."

I'm holding a compress hard against the long scratch on Grace's leg.

"It hurts, Mommy!" Grace says.

Lynne stops what she's doing and turns her face so she's looking right at me. Not nicely. She gives Grace a quick hug, then says, "I'm going to look for that form in my office."

Dad always tries to distract me when I'm upset. It annoys me, but I can't think of anything else to do now than talk. "You know, Grace, I was thinking about some-thing you said to me. About putting dandelions in balloons and getting two wishes. Maybe we could do that one day."

"That's unpossible," Faith says.

"Maybe," I say. "But we can try. Would you like that, Grace?"

She nods. "And maybe we could blow a bubble around the dandelion and put both in the balloon."

Faith shakes her head. "You can't. That's stupid."

I pick the compress off Grace's leg and the bleeding has almost completely stopped. The cut, which had looked raging and angry, has softened to pink. "I'm okay, Marley. I'm just gonna tell Mommy I'm okay now."

I step into the bathroom. I wash my hands and sit on the closed toilet seat for what feels like an inappropriately long time. Lynne seemed a little over the edge. I guess parents can get crazy protective when their children are hurt. Well, some parents. My dad hasn't shown too many signs of that animal instinct this summer.

When I come out, Lynne says, "She's had her shots. Marley, can I trust you to keep them away from that table in the future?"

To which I would like to reply, *Do you think it is the best idea to have a rusting metal table in your own backyard?* But of course I don't say anything. That's my specialty.

* * *

When I walk into my dad's after work, I want to lie down and try to sleep through most of the rest of the day or summer, but the message light's flashing. A lot. I'm pressing the button as Dad comes into the room.

It's Mom's voice. "Robert. Are you there? Please pick up." A surge of homesickness swells in my chest. "I'll call back." Then a click. Another click—a hang-up.

"Robert? You know, you really need a cell phone. It's Wednesday morning and the surgery is over. I think everything is going to be fine. I really do. Mom lost a lot of blood but they say that's not unusual. It's just hard to see her so weak. And she can't get a transfusion until tomorrow at the earliest." My mother makes some weird noise that I think is a stifled cry, then says, "I'm really okay," and clicks down the phone.

Dad looks at me, waiting to see if I'm going to explode.

I sit down on the couch. I feel nauseated, like something thick is stuck in my throat.

"Can I call Mom?"

"I'm sure she'll call when she knows something."

I sit on the floor and Rig comes right over. He presses his head into my chest and I rub his ears.

The thought of my grandmother all, I don't know, weak and old, and my mother feeling sad, it just makes me want to pound things.

"We should go to the hospital," I say.

"What?" Dad calls from the kitchen.

"I said that we should go to the hospital, right? Isn't that what we should do?"

"I don't think so, Marley."

I do. I very much do.

Weird feelings are racing around and they're all telling me one thing—I need to be there. The pain and fear and sadness inside me remind me of that big hole I felt when my mother left me at preschool. But this time, I'm old enough to do something about it. I need to get to the hospital and see them. It's weird, but it's a real physical need, like thirst.

But this is another one of those Dad things. He's going to want to do things his way, or the way he thinks they should be, without listening to what I want. And he has a long history of vetoing every request I make.

I will wait until I can figure out a way to make him understand.

But I need to do something now. I go in my room and make my bed, even though it's afternoon. I brush my hair and my teeth. I look around my room and pick a piece of dust off the floor. What am I doing?

I check for messages—nothing.

I text Leah. No answer.

I take Rig outside. It's cloudy and hot, and I just sit there, looking at the back of Jack's house. Rig walks a circle around me and settles at my feet.

I don't know what to do. I don't feel like I can trust myself to even talk without bursting into tears. Who would I talk to anyway? Leah's been blowing me off. I will not even mention Jane. I blew it with Jack, or maybe he blew it with me, but it doesn't really matter who blew it because there's nobody.

I don't have anyone.

"Marley!" My dad's calling me from the back door. "Your mom's on the phone!"

"Come on, Rig," I say. He just looks at me, then closes his eyes. "Fine."

Dad's holding the door open. "Is everything okay?" I say to him. He just puts the phone in my hand.

"Mom!"

"Hey there, my girl," Mom says. Her voice is so tired and so sad that my stomach drops. Mom's an only child, like me, dealing with all of this by herself.

"What's going on? How's Grandma?"

"I'm not sure yet, to tell you the truth, honey. I think it will be fine. She lost a lot of blood, but they don't seem too concerned. They say it happens a lot."

"Can I come visit her?"

"Not yet. Definitely not now."

"I want to. I want to see her. I want to see you."

"I'll tell you what. Let's talk again tomorrow. Maybe she'll be doing better."

"I wish I were there, Mom. I really do."

"I know, Marley. I miss you."

"I miss you too."

I wait until I hang up to start crying. It's automatic, and I don't even bother trying to hold it in. I don't want my father's comfort right now, so I go out back where he won't hear me. And there's Jack, rubbing Rig's stomach.

"Marley?"

"Oh, God." I cover my eyes with my hands. No. No, no, no, no. Jack is not seeing me like this. Please. How much worse is life going to get? I'm snorfling and disgusting and I have no tissues and I desperately need tissues. "I'm a mess," I say.

He looks at me, his eyes filled with something that looks like pain. "Oh," he says. "Uh. What can I . . . um, hmm. Wanna walk?"

I nod. He takes my hand and leads me to the front of his house.

Oh my God. I'm miserable and I'm crying but holy oly oly crap! Jack's holding my hand. Did I wipe snot on it? Oh God, let me not have wiped snot on it. My God, Jack's hand! His hand is in my hand. Oh! But no.

My grandmother. I can't.

I need to go to sleep and wake up in a few weeks. When this is all over. When it's already better.

Except right now, I'm holding Jack's hand.

"Hey, look at that," he says. Stuck in the hedges that line the walk from Jack's house to the street are three Opportunity Knocks cards and Baltic (Baltic: just relax). Jack gathers them and brings them to the trash can.

We walk down the block and across the street. Rig remembers the tree house and settles himself at the bottom. I know I have to let go of Jack's hand to climb up the ladder, but I'd pay significant cash to hold on. I even like the feel of the calluses where his fingers meet his palm. I let go and climb up.

I breathe in the old rot smell.

Jack asks, "Just . . . is there anything I can do?"

I shake my head.

"I'm so sorry, Marley. I acted like an idiot. I should have just shut up."

Because of the strange mechanics of laughing and crying at the same time, I snort.

"You snort?"

"Not usually." I'm almost laughing and then I'm back to crying. There has never been a bigger mess than Marley Baird, one summer night in a house atop the trees. "My grandmother is going to be fine, so I don't really know why I'm crying. I snorted because that's why I'm crying. Not because you were an idiot." It occurs to me that I may be lacking a basic filter that would keep me from saying things that other people have the sense to just think. "Sorry," I say.

"No, I was an idiot. You needed to figure stuff out. I was just pissed about a lot of my own things and it all came, I don't know, like shooting out of me. I'm really sorry."

"I'm sorry too. I was kind of crazy that night. I shouldn't have been so pissy at you. I've missed you," I say, then wonder if I can get that filter installed somehow. A person ought to be able to think things without blurting them.

"I felt like I dented our friendship or something." He shakes his head.

I start crying again.

"So is it bad? Is your grandmother really sick? Or hurt?"

"It was just an operation and she lost a lot of blood but honestly, it doesn't seem like it's going to be bad— I think she'll be fine—so don't ask why I'm crying because I have no idea."

He's looking at me with such soft eyes, with some kind of gentle warmth behind them. He's listening. He's more than listening. It's like he's feeling what I'm saying.

It occurs to me that I'm showing Jack who I am right now, the worst of who I am. The part of me I should be working hardest to hide. The force of all that's happening is as hard and fast as a bigtime waterfall— not the kind of thing that's easy to stop.

The tears are threatening to start up again. "Hey, Jack? Could we talk about something else?"

"Sure," he says.

"Have you heard from Will?"

He presses his lips together and shakes his head. "It's not easy to stay friends when you can't hang out, you know?"

"I'm not sure it's easy to stay friends even when you can." He looks at me for a second as though I've lost him, but then he gets it. As if I willed him along in the conversation. "Your friend Leah, right?"

"Yeah."

"Oh, I meant to tell you. I saw her at the park. She was riding her bike when I was working on some drills with the little kids. We talked for a little while. I know things are, like, wobbly with you guys, but she does seem pretty cool. Maybe you guys can work it out."

I wish I were Rig right now. He does this thing when two people he loves stand too near each other—he tries to put himself between them. He'll push his nose between their legs and start pushing his body through. Then he'll keep working his way, around the legs and back through, like a psycho cat playing London Bridge. Usually he gets his way. The two people—it used to mostly be my mom and dad—will separate and hug him and laugh until he's thumping out happy sounds with his leg or tail.

I want to do the human equivalent of that to Jack and Leah. I want to separate them—to force myself between them and physically push them apart from each other. There's no denying that Leah is way more attractive than I am—she has that wavy hair, and her crazy-long legs are impossible not to notice. I'll bet Jack just thinks of me as a friend, a Yankees pal, but sees Leah as potentially something else. I can just picture him asking me for advice about her. Shoot me.

"You keep going quiet," Jack says. "You okay?"

I nod. I don't know what to say. I want to ask him: *Were you happy to see her? Why was she there? Did she say anything about me?* All these feelings—the *Won't you please still be my friend even though I'm not sure I like you anymore?* feelings I have toward Leah, and the *You like me more than you like her, right?* feelings that are scratching toward the surface with Jack—just make me hate myself.

He's quiet too. Of course he is. Here I am, speaking Sad Freaked-Out Girl to him. Again. Have I not learned that this part of me is repellant?

And what kind of person is even thinking about her own problems when her grandmother is in the hospital?

"Jack, what's that?" I'm pointing at a collection of . . . something. In the corner of the tree house.

"Not telling," he says, half laughing. Half embarrassed, maybe?

"Oh, you're telling," I say, and I start to scoot over to the corner. He tries to grab my ankle, but I yank it free. "Water balloons?"

He looks like he wants to hide. "I . . . hmm. Well, I

couldn't decide if this was a really good idea or a terrible one, but I thought that if you were walking by one day or something, maybe I'd—"

"Attack me? Blitz me? Seriously?" I'm trying to remember how much I told him about that awful night. Could he really not know what a terrible idea that is? Just holding one brings back the night in full-color detail. High-definition humiliation.

"Like an icebreaker? I thought maybe that was what we needed. You would laugh. Or yell at me. Or throw a few back up."

I just sit there, squeezing the balloon a little.

"Are you going to throw that at my head, or just sit there squeezing it?" he asks.

"Not sure yet."

The feel of that water balloon brings it all back.

I wish I could do the whole thing over. I could not go to that party. That would have probably been the smartest thing.

Except it wouldn't have mattered.

I didn't know it then—and I'm still trying to get it, absorb it, *really* know it now—but it was already over with me and Leah and Jane anyway. All I did with that blitz was let them think it was all my fault.

It's so quiet, but my thoughts feel loud. Before I

end up blurting something I'll regret, I say, "I should go home in case my mom calls again."

We climb down the ladder and Rig's tail thumps the ground.

We walk without talking. At the exact spot where our backyards meet, Jack takes my hand again. "Good night," he says. "Can I just . . ." And then he stops talking. He leans in and down and kisses my cheek quickly. He smells like almond soap. His lips are dry and just touch my skin lightly, gently, deliciously. His fingers briefly glide through my hair, brushing aside everything. He turns and walks across his yard and into his house. I catch my breath, make sure my legs still work, and walk slowly home.

Even the Silences

The next morning I call my mother's cell phone and, miraculously, she answers. "Did she have the transfusion? Is she better?"

"I don't know, Marley. I'm still at her house. I came back to sleep for a little while. I'm just out the door now."

"I really want to visit. I mean, maybe Grandma would want to see me, right? And I want to see her. I want to be there, and see her and see you, and—"

"Why don't you let me see how she is today, okay? I miss you too. It would help to see you now."

That makes me all weepy.

My life must be officially turned upside down, because instead of dreading work, I'm almost looking forward to seeing Grace and Faith today.

I decide to spring the question on Dad in the truck, on the way to the Krolls'. I know he'll say no, that he has to cut lawns and it's serious business, Marley! But I am determined to fight this battle until I win. I don't know why I need to see Grandma—but I know that I do. I need to visit her and I need to see my mother. It's just about the only thing I've been sure about all summer.

Dad completely zags where I knew he would zig. "Anything you want, Marley."

I'm about to start yelling, to begin my begging, but wait—what?

"When your grandmother's well enough to see you, I'll get you there."

"Really?"

"There are lots of things we have no control over. This is not one of those things. If what you need is to be with your mom and to see your grandmother, I can help you with that. I want to help you with that."

"Thank you," I say, the tears right back at the corners of my eyes.

* * *

The girls must have some kind of sense, because they're mellower than they've ever been. They spend half the morning playing hairdresser, with me as their client.

"Would you like a twist?"

"Kwee wet your hair?"

I let them do anything they want to my hair as long as it doesn't involve scissors. As I sit there, their chubby little-kid hands all over my head, I worry about Grandma. And occasionally, the memory of that kiss pops in my mind too, demanding attention.

A kiss from Jack sounds like such a magical combination of four words.

I try like crazy to think only of those four words, but three other words have a weight all their own. *On. The. Cheek.* A kiss from Jack! On the cheek. Like the caboose, pulled inevitably along, impossible to leave behind.

When the twins get tired of my hair, Faith goes to a drawer, pulls something out, and drops it in my lap. A bag of balloons. Ugh, balloons. Thanks, Faith. I think briefly of the stash in the tree house and I almost laugh.

What if I *had* been walking by and Jack blitzed me? Would I have laughed or burst into tears? How can I not know the answer to that question?

"Kwee do that thing with the two wishes?" Grace asks. "We tried and it didn't work. Kwee do that now and you help us?"

I feel a little too broken to do this, but I stand, and we go outside to hunt dandelions. The twins find a ton, but it turns out that it's no easy feat to shove a dandelion into a balloon without ruining the dandelion. Or tearing the balloon.

But if you blow up the balloon a little, and then stretch out the part you blow into, you can shove them inside.

Not neatly.

After lots of failed attempts, we succeed. Sort of. I blow up the balloon and hand it to Grace. She closes her eyes for a long time, then lets go of the balloon. It drops to the ground.

"It's not flying away, Marley Bear," Grace says.

"I knew that wouldn't work none," Faith says.

"Yeah, but it looks cool, right?" I'm trying. I don't have much, but I'm trying. I knew they wouldn't float away without helium, but I figured, she's five. Maybe just having it in the balloon would be enough.

"We could smash it," Faith says. "That's the best about balloons anyway, smashing them."

"Really?" I've always hated the sound of balloons popping. I thought all kids did.

Grace is trying to get her dandelion balloon to take off—throwing it, going on the swing with it to launch it. Faith stays back, trying to explain. "It's the *popping*," she says, a big *DUH* in her tone. "The sitting on or smashing or stomping on them? It's good for when you're mad."

"Really?"

She nods. "Yeah. It's good to smash stuff. With balloons, you don't get in trouble." I can see how balloons could be a good smashing alternative to your sister's toys and your mother's fragile china.

"I could use some smashing," I say. "Let's blow all these balloons up and smash them."

"YES!" Faith says. "Come on, Grace, we're gonna pop 'em all."

"Not all. Not mine."

"Okay," I say. "Come pop these other ones with us. It's going to be fun."

We get a big pile ready, and then we jump on them. We sit on them. We scream as they pop, and scream when they squeak out from underneath us without popping, and then we hunt them down and pop them for real. It's loud and it's fantastic.

* * *

Lynne brings us to the park in the afternoon and then picks the girls up early. Grace and Faith and I make it through the whole day without fighting.

As soon as they pull out of the parking lot, I use my cell phone to check my dad's messages. Mom hasn't called. I can't stand the waiting. I walk over to the baseball fields, sit on a bench, and watch, my fingers picking at the chipping paint on the seat.

There are maybe forty kids here, and most of them seem little. They're all mixed in together, playing games.

They break up to do throwing drills, run the bases, and hit the ball off a tee. Jack doesn't seem to be practicing so much himself as he is helping all the little kids. He walks over when a kid's at bat to push his feet into the right position and lift his bat off his shoulder. He crouches down as a catcher when a kid wants to practice her pitching.

I feel someone sit on the bench next to me. "Hey," she says. "Marley. We meet again."

"Oh, hey, Callie. What's up?" I haven't seen her since the Fourth. I sort of never want to see anyone from that party ever again, but Callie's cool.

"Not much," she says. "You have a little brother or something in the camp?"

"Me? No. I'm just waiting for my friend Jack."

"Oh, Jack."

"You know him?"

"In an *oh, hi* way, you know?"

"Yeah."

"Hey, Marley. Did something happen at Jane's party? I thought I saw you go, and I wanted to call to see if everything was okay, but—"

"It was no big deal," I say. "It was just time to go."

She shrugs. "How's your summer been?"

"Not so great," I say. "I'm babysitting these twins, so I have no free time." I could go on—the list of things that aren't so great is really kind of impressive—but Callie and I don't have enough history for me to just rant on.

"I know what you mean. My mother has me in charge of bringing Brian here and picking him up." She rolls her eyes.

I'm thinking that leaves her whole days free, but

she's looking for co-misery, not a pep talk. "Are you do-ing anything else?"

"Actually, my family is going to Vermont next Fri-day for two weeks. It's where my dad grew up. How 'bout you?"

"I'm staying with my dad. Just hanging, I guess." I could impress her with my big hoped-for trip—to visit my grandmother in the hospital—but I wouldn't want to make Callie jealous.

A coach or someone walks toward the main field's pitcher's mound and blows a whistle, and everyone at once starts to gather up equipment. Moms and a few dads are waiting in the parking lot, some in their cars, some talking in small groups. A little kid, maybe nine, walks over to Callie. "You have fun, Brian?" she asks.

He grunts, "Yeh."

"I have to get the runt home," she says, her hand on top of the cap on his head. "Maybe I'll see you around."

"Yeah, give me a call when you're back from Ver-mont," I surprise myself by saying.

"I need your number," she says. We add our num-bers to each other's phones before Callie leaves with her brother.

My life was all Leah and Jane for so long. No thinking, no planning—just my go-to girls. It has been so long since I've hung out with anyone else. Just the thought of a new friend has the sort of glow that good ideas have. Maybe it'll be good and fun and new. I could use some good. And fun. And new.

The clump of kids on the field gets smaller until it's Jack and a few little ones. He seems to see me, then moves his head to get a better look. He waves, then holds up his index finger: one minute. He waits until all the kids have left, then trots over to me, his big bag banging the backs of his legs. "You look like Little Bo Peep who lost her sheep."

"Really?"

"Where's your twins?"

"Their mom picked them up a little while ago. I got a tiny bit of freedom."

"And you chose to sit here and watch my camp?"

I think of the *Busted!* look Rig gets when I catch him doing something wrong. "Do you know Callie Larson?" I say. "I was just waiting with her until her brother was done. Brian, I think."

Nice, Marley. Nice.

"Callie! I always forget her name. I keep thinking it's Lassie, and that's not right."

"Not at all."

"Yeah, I'm friends with the guy she goes out with. He goes to Little Valley."

"Ethan?"

"Yeah."

I want to keep talking about Callie, like a kindergartener who made a new friend at school. I'm kind of humming with the excitement of it.

Jack packs up all the equipment and waves to some coach out in the outfield. We start walking toward home.

"Oh," Jack says. "I forgot to ask you. Are we good for Sunday?"

"What?"

"The Yankees game. Dean said he'd pick us up from the stadium, take us out to dinner afterward, and drive us home. We could take the train up. It's an afternoon game."

Whoa. Will Dad let me do this? Must answer. Must not allow silence to grow longer. Marley, *TALK*. "Yeah, right. I just have to check with my dad."

I picture myself sitting in a baseball stadium next to Jack for three hours. I wonder if he asked me because he thinks I'm a huge Yankees fan. Or was that kiss on the cheek more than an *I'm sorry your grandmother's sick, friend* thing? Is it a date? My brain feels like it's making that bad sound a hard drive makes when it's working too hard.

* * *

Dad calls to say he's going to be working late, that he spoke to my mom, and that we can visit on Sunday. Sunday! I tell him about the Yankee game and ask if it's anywhere near the hospital, if it'll work out timing wise and if it would be okay, and he says we can talk about it when he gets home.

I make myself some macaroni and cheese and bring it to the coffee table. I'm about to settle down in front of the TV when I hear Rig's *May I please go outside now?* "Ruh."

"Just a sec," I yell to him.

I bring the food back to the kitchen, grab my sandals, and take him out the back door.

Rig shoots outside and races over to Jack, who's standing next to someone. In fact, the someone is practically on top of him. That someone is Leah, with one hand on her hip. With the other hand she keeps flipping her hair in this really annoying way that she's been doing since fifth grade. It's the patented Leah Stamnick Flirty Hair Flip.

"Marley," she says, and I can feel it coming, the tide of bad luck turned right back on me. "I didn't know you were such a big Yankees fan! You'd think I'd know such a thing, being your friend since second grade."

I know it's illegal, and also just wrong on a lot of levels, to kill another person. Still, I want to kill her. I do.

"It's something I've sort of always shared with my dad. We listen to games together all the time." There's something absurd and defensive in my voice.

"Oh, really," she says, with yet another Leah Stamnick Flirty Hair Flip.

"It's not exactly something you and I would discuss, since you hate baseball," I say. "What are you doing here? And why did you blow me off on Saturday?"

"I was riding by and I saw Jack out here all by himself and thought I'd stop by and say hello." At this moment, I can't really remember anything I ever liked about her. I see all her bad parts squeezing out: flirty here, untrustworthy there, dishonest over there.

"So," she says, her hand reaching out for Jack's arm. "Hello!"

Even from this distance across the yard, I can see that he's smiling.

"Don't you have some scripts you should be reading?" I ask. Leah looks at me for a second, like a bewildered animal, and then my dad's phone starts ringing inside. I want to run back in the house. I also want to make sure Leah doesn't jump on top of Jack. I have that same urge of wanting to put myself between them, or sending Rig to do the job with his psycho-kitty-separation-of-people-standing-too-close-routine. I say, "I have to get the phone," and go back inside.

It's my mom. "Hey, honey, how are you doing?"

"Okay," I say.

"What's wrong?"

"Oh, Leah's just . . . I don't know. Anyway, I think I'm coming to see you and Grandma on Sunday, right?"

"That'll be great. I forgot to ask your dad if he would do me a favor."

"What?"

"I didn't realize how long I'd be staying up here, so I didn't pack enough. Do you think you and Dad could go over to the house and bring me some clothes? And I'm going to need my folder of registration forms for work. They're on the left side of my desk, under that big book. Just grab some shirts and pants, maybe a sundress or something?"

"Sure."

"That would be great, save me a trip. Thanks, Marley. Thank your dad for me too. I'll see you on Sunday at the hospital, then."

"Wait! Mom. How is she?"

"She's still weak, but they say that's normal. She smiled when I said you'd be coming to see her."

"Is her hip better? Did the operation fix her hip?"

"It should be . . ." She stops. "I'm sorry," she says.

Maybe we both just have some constant crying disease. And maybe someday it will go away. I hate this. "Give Grandma a kiss from me, okay?"

"I will. Be good, honey."

Like I'm five. "Okay. I love you."

"You too. Bye."

I go back to the window and stand by it (actually, a little under it), spying on Jack and Leah. I see her throw her head back in that flirty laughing way, at the same time she puts her hand on Jack's arm and moves it down about six inches, like she's feeling his muscle. A whole new move, as yet unpatented and unnamed.

It's better not to watch. I know this, but I continue to look. At some point, though, I just go back into the kitchen and warm up the macaroni and cheese. I bring it into the living room to eat. I click on the remote as the doorbell rings.

"Ruh ruh ruh ruh ruh ruh ruh ruh ruh." I hear Rig, but where is he?

"I'm coming," I say.

Baseball noises from the TV fill the room. Dad was up late last night, watching the game. Did he forget his key? Why is he ringing the bell?

I open the door. It's Jack. And Rig. "Ruh," Rig says.

"Hey," Jack says. "You forgot your dog. I like how he barks from either side of the door when the bell rings."

"Why are you at the front door?"

"I tried willing you to come out the back, but you never did. So can I come in?"

"Of course. I was just eating," I say, leading Jack into the house.

"Oh, I'm sorry—"

"No, it's, like, mac and cheese. No big deal. Want some?"

"Sure, why not?" He sits on the couch. "Cool. What's the score?"

"I just turned it on," I say, going into the kitchen to warm up more food. "What do you want to drink?"

"Do you have any orange juice?"

"Yeah, but my dad keeps buying the kind with pulp."

"I like pulp."

"Are you serious?"

"Totally."

It's so weird, making a guy dinner in my dad's kitchen. I've never done anything like this. It seems a little too good to be really happening. I half expect the doorbell to ring again and for Leah to say she was just passing by and happened to catch a whiff and she's so hungry and would I mind?

But I guess Leah must have left. I want to ask what they talked about. But I decide to try to just be happy that he's here. I'm relieved too, after everything, that he's choosing to spend time with me. I bring out another bowl of macaroni and cheese, a fork, and a glass of pulpy orange juice. We start to eat, watching the game. We talk a little, but our silences are fine too, part of the new dialect we're creating together.

When Dad gets home, he sits in the chair across from the couch. I'm wondering if he'll be cool with me and Jack just being here by ourselves. It's not like we've done anything. But this hasn't exactly come up before, me and a guy hanging out by ourselves in an empty house.

His eyes still on the TV, Dad asks Jack, "Did you know last night's game went to thirteen innings?"

"And hello to you," I say.

Dad smiles at me.

"And then the Yanks gave up that home run in the top of the thirteenth," Jack says.

"We'll get 'em tonight," Dad says. "What's the score?"

"Four-two, us," I say. Us. Like we're all on the same team. "Hey, Dad? Mom wants us to go over to the house and get some clothes to bring to her on Sunday. Do you have time to do that after work tomorrow?"

"Sure." Dad says, folding up some paper. He stands and takes it to the blue recycling container by the back door. "Jack, what do you know about the bulk trash pickup around here?" Dad is looking out the window at his tower of cartons. He looks twitchy, like old Dad is taking over the new him.

"Sorry, I don't know anything. And I've gotta get home," Jack says. "Oh, did you ask about the game?"

"She did," my dad says. "I wasn't clear on the details." And so they talk about times and seat locations and how Dean is going to pick us up. "I can't be sure what time I'll get Marley there," my dad tells Jack. "Why don't you give her the ticket so she can meet you at the seats?"

"Good idea," Jack says.

"How are you getting to the game?" my dad asks. It

feels like some kind of old sitcom. Like he's asking about his intentions, only in code or something.

"Train, then subway," he says.

"Nothing like the train," Dad says.

"Nothing like the train," Jack says.

Dad walks into the kitchen. I hear him banging around the pot and colander, which I didn't clean. Or put away.

"Would it be okay if I look at the middle bedroom?" Jack asks. "I want to see what Will's room looks like post-Will."

We walk down the hall to my room. "He had a poster of Babe Ruth on the back of the door, there, and a dartboard with the Red Sox logo right in the middle of the bull's-eye."

"Cool," I say. My dad hates the Red Sox too. It's what Yankees fans do.

There's something swirly in my stomach, like my body just realized I'm alone in my bedroom with Jack. I'm dizzy. Jack's fingers are grazing the top of my blanket. Whoa. I think I might explode. How do you keep yourself from exploding? I really don't want to explode in front of Jack.

"Hey, Marley?" my dad calls from the kitchen. I don't know if he's sensing something about how long we've been in my room together, like some kind of protective dad radar, but for once his timing doesn't suck.

"I'm gonna go," Jack says.

Explosion averted.

"Wait," he says. "Can I have your cell number?"

"Yeah," I write the number and watch him fold it and stuff it deep into his pocket.

"See ya Sunday," Jack says.

In two more days, Jack will be in his personal nirvana: Yankee Stadium. And I will be in mine: next to Jack.

Forever Changes

There's a tower of mail on the floor, piled up from the mailman pushing it through the slot. The house is warm with the heavy air of a place that has been closed up for a while. The smell and the feel and just the sight of everything familiar to me bring on a wave of painful homesickness for all that's lost—my friends, the way I lived comfortably in one home and didn't have to constantly readjust to the other. Even in the midst of this overwhelming longing, though, is the tickle of knowledge that back then, when all that other good stuff was still in place, I didn't know that there was a Jack-with-light-blue-eyes out there. A Jack I look forward to seeing every morning.

I grab piles of mail and stack them semi-neatly on the coffee table. When I look up, my dad's hand is on a picture frame on the bookshelf, and the look in his eyes betrays something close to what I'm feeling (without the Jack part). I step behind him. It's a picture of the three of us—Mom, Dad, and me—on vacation in Bermuda when I was two. I'm sitting, my fat baby legs covered in sand, with Mom and Dad leaning toward each other right behind me, smiling. I don't remember the trip, but that picture has been on that shelf forever. My parents look like younger, happier versions of their present selves.

Dad smiles. "That was a great trip," he says.

We stand there just looking at that picture for a long time, until I say, "I'll go get Mom's stuff."

I go to my room first. Oh, my room. My books! My stuff! On the shelves, framed pictures of—ugh—Leah and Jane and me everywhere. I sit on my bed and feel that no-glasses Jane staring at me. I stay there a few minutes and try not to feel, not to think. It's impossible.

In my mom's room, I'm hit with another ache. I miss my mom!

I've never been away from her for this long before. I open her drawers and just touch her clothes. I try to remember which pants she likes to wear with which shirts, but all her clothes look foreign to me. I take a couple of pairs of capris and some T-shirts, grab some underwear and a couple of nightgowns, and throw it all into her old overnight bag. I look in the bathroom for anything she might want.

"Dad?"

"Yeah?"

"Is there anything you can think of that I should bring besides clothes?"

"There's a jasmine spray that she keeps in her night table drawer. She sprays it on her pillow to help her sleep. If it's in there, maybe you could grab that."

It's exactly where he said it would be. I spray it in the air. Its sweetness is the smell of my mother. I hadn't known that came from a little plastic bottle. I go in her closet and pull out a couple of dresses, then close the bedroom door behind me. In the office, I find the file of new-student registration forms under her big book.

I carry her packed bag into the living room, but I don't want to leave my house yet.

"You okay?" Dad says.

I nod, then shake my head. "It's hard," I say, the

familiar burn of tears in my eyes at the kindness in his. "And I'm so sick of crying all the time." It's as though there is some secret cue and I just hit it on the mark, because as I say that, the tears leave the starting position and take off down my face.

"Oh, Marley. I know." Dad reaches out his left arm to me and pulls me against his chest. "It is hard. It's all hard."

I cry for a while. I wish Rig were here. Whenever I cry, he walks over, slowly, and when he can no longer wait, he licks my face. When I was younger, I believed it was out of compassion, but I've learned that he cannot resist the taste of salt.

When I get my breathing back, I ask, "Do you really get that? How hard it all is? Do you have any idea of what's going on? Like how my friends aren't my friends anymore and how I don't want to go back to school because how do you go to school when you have no friends? It's, like, impossible."

"Your mother's been gone. Your grandmother's sick. You're living in two different places. I think I get it."

It feels like that earthquake movie set is splitting inside me, knocking the sadness off-balance and replacing it with this big, red, angry wave of something else.

"And do you also get how all this started when you moved out?" My tone is not one either of us is used to.

He's silent. For a long time.

My tears are still coming, but they're furious, not sad.

Dad reaches close, the smell of shaving cream and cut grass, and he tries to put his arms around me. No. I don't want that. I stand up and stalk around the living room.

"Is there one thing that's bothering you the most?" His voice is quiet, controlled.

Most? When everything sucks so completely, do I really need to prioritize all the things that are wrong? I have no friends. I keep slipping back and forth between two homes; and I can't get my footing anywhere.

"It's everything," I say finally. The truth. "It's you, and it's my friends, or my not-friends. My not-friends and my not-family."

"Let's start out easy." His voice is infuriatingly calm. My fists and teeth are clenched, and my head is throbbing. "How can you start to make things better with Leah and Jane?"

"I can't. I don't even trust them. Like, at all. I don't even like them anymore."

"Do you remember what I told you about Babe Ruth and Lou Gehrig? Did you think at all about that?"

As if everything should have been solved with his wise baseball story. "That was about some little misunderstanding. This is about friends who aren't treating me right. Friends who turned out to not be the best of people."

"You'll meet new people," he says.

"You don't understand: I've been friends with Leah and Jane forever. It's impossible to start over."

"Forever changes," Dad says. "I thought your mom and I would be married forever. It's normal for relationships to change. Sometimes people change, and they grow apart. It's not bad or wrong. It just happens."

"You know what, Dad? I am so sick of that, how it's no one's fault and blah blah blah. Because really? I think it is someone's fault. I think Leah and Jane could have been better friends to me. I think it *is* their fault. And I think you and Mom could have fixed it before it broke. And I don't think it's normal for you to be going out with Lynne already. You don't seem to realize how totally and completely this sucks for me. Except for Grandma, you've said no to, like, everything all summer, and—"

"Hold it," he says. "What are you talking about?"

"When I wanted to quit—and I *really* wanted to quit—you said no. When I wanted my computer at your house, you said no."

"You're missing something, pal," he says. "I've been saying it over and over, but you're still missing it. We're in a new place now. We do not have the same kind of spending money we had before. I keep saying it's the economic reality of a two-household family."

He's right. He has been saying that over and over. And I never really bothered to think past the big Dad words. It just sounded like some excuse.

"Okay, so that's the Internet fee, fine. But about the twins—" And I feel stupid even saying that, because I don't feel the same dread about them now that I used to. What I want isn't to get away from them, but maybe to help them at least a tiny bit, the way I wish someone would help me.

I sit down next to him.

"I figured you'd want spending money this summer. To do things. I don't have a lot of extra cash. It's the economic reality—"

"Okay, I get it," I say, but I almost wish that I didn't.

"I want to tell you one more thing," he says, his voice low. He pushes my hair away from my face, the way he's done since I was three. "I'm sorry that you've been hurt by this. I want you to know that I'm hurting too. I miss the way we were. And I'll miss seeing you every day. I ache for that too. But I also know that I have to move on."

We sit there, all those words swirling around us. Whatever anger I felt has melted into sadness. And a little bit of shame.

He squeezes my knee and says, "I know you will find your way through this. I really believe that."

He waits a little longer before he asks, "Are you ready to go now?"

I am. So we do.

When we're driving past the old park, we get stopped at the endless red light. I look over to the park entrance where Leah and Jane and I used to meet on our bikes. There's no one there now.

We drive on.

Something Good Will Grow in Its Place

In the morning, I'm still heavy with the sadness of last night. I grab Dad's dandelion tool and choose a new patch of lawn, near the holes I made last time, and I begin again. He made good progress with his various concoctions, but a few have come back. I stand for leverage, then reach in and pull out the remaining white root.

"Morning, Marley," Jack says.

"Hey, Jack."

"So what is it, exactly, that you're doing here? I've

been watching you make holes in your dad's lawn for a long time now, and I'm not sure I'm getting it."

"My father is a dandelion hater."

"No shame in that."

"He hasn't had the time to deal with them." I think about the days when we worked side by side cleaning up the lawn, a perfectly nice time. Then yesterday I howled at him like an angry wolf-child and revealed myself to be a spoiled brat.

"Isn't there some kind of spray or something?"

"There is, but he won't use anything like that. He's organic." I say that word with something like ridicule in my voice, but I have no idea why, as I totally respect that part of my dad. I love that he's committed to organic gardening.

"Will you ever really be done? It seems like you make all these holes and then the next day there's just more weeds growing back."

"I know. But I'm starting to think that once you dig out the weed, there's at least a chance that something good will grow in its place."

He shrugs and smiles. "What time do you think you'll get to the game tomorrow?"

"I'm not even sure what time visiting hours are. What time are you leaving?"

"I'm going up early. I spoke to my brother. He's meeting us at the McDonald's across the street at four thirty. What're you doing today?"

"I'm not sure. What about you?"

"Some guys are getting together to practice for try-outs. I'm going to head over to my friend Justin's and play. Oh, here," he says, handing me the ticket for to-morrow's game. "I'll see you there."

"Thanks." The feeling I get when Jack reaches down for his bag, the sign that he's going to leave, re-minds me of those stories Mom told about my morn-ings at nursery school, how I wrapped my arms around her legs. *Oh, please. Stay with me.*

* * *

Dad spends hours at Home Depot. In the afternoon I find a fresh bagel—sesame, my favorite kind—from the best shop in town waiting for me on the table. Not quite a gesture, maybe, but it was nice of him.

He eats his dinner in front of the TV. I take two really long walks with Rig and finish reading a thick novel.

* * *

That night, Leah texts me.

Whats up?

Just hanging. U?

Not much. Hanging with Jane.

Ok. TTYL.

What happened at library?

Nothing. Gotta go.

I tried talking to her 4 u.

Oh no. No she didn't. NO!

I told you not to.

Doesn't matter. She doesn't wan

That text comes through cut off. And then—

This is Jane.

I turn off my phone fast, like it's a bomb.

Why would Leah . . . I'm panting. Why am I panting?

Why would Leah do this? Why did she have to turn our slightly messed-up two-person friendship into some kind of Leah and Jane thing? She promised not to do this.

The very far reaches of the farthest part of the back of my brain know that Leah just gave me the answer to a question I haven't yet had the nerve to ask: Do I try to work things out with her?

I cannot trust her. At all.

I liked her once.

We used to have so much fun.

But I do not like her now.

So why haven't I already walked away from Leah in a big and final way?

The answer, once I find it, is awful.

I don't want to be alone.

I don't want to be the girl with no one to sit with in the cafeteria.

It's a horrid, lonely truth.

I want to ignore the question that's lined up right behind it: What kind of person pretends to be friends with someone just to save herself from being alone?

I don't know the answer yet, but I'm scared the answer is me.

* * *

Grandma lives pretty far away, and the hospital is near her house. The drive is long and familiar and boring. Dad listens to a news radio station because he wants to hear all the traffic reports. I beg him to put on one of my CDs, but he doesn't relent until we've been in the car for way more than an hour. It's as painful and boring as fishing, only without the good, open air.

I spend way too much time thinking about that awful text from Leah, and that one from Jane. I work up the nerve to check if they kept texting me after I turned my phone off. No. Nothing.

Dad stops for breakfast at a diner, and we talk about the Yankees and he somehow gets me to agree to go fishing with him next weekend. I'm so scared that he's going to do the *I listen* Dad routine and ask me to talk about my anger, revisit all the things I said Friday night. He doesn't. Maybe he's relieved at not having to go near all that stuff again today. I know I am.

* * *

The hospital itself is kind of depressing, which isn't altogether surprising, since it's a hospital. It's smaller than I imagined—a square yellow brick building surrounded by asphalt parking lots.

Dad talks to someone at a desk in the lobby and we're directed through a maze of hallways that seem longer than the building looked from the outside. We find the elevator and ride up to the fifth floor. When the doors open, an awful smell greets us. I don't even want to think too much about what it is, but it's truly horrible.

We walk down the hall toward room 517. Dad steps in first. There's an empty bed near the door, then a curtain. On the other side of the room, near the window, there's Grandma, sleeping.

Her mouth is open and kind of drooping. As we walk in, closer, I can see that there's an IV tube connected to the top of her hand, where it's taped on. And a whole horror show of beeping, lit-up machines attached to different parts of her.

Mom is sitting in a big chair on the other side of the bed, looking up at a TV. "Deb," Dad says, and she stands immediately. She hugs him quickly and then rushes over to me and pulls me to her in a big hug. It reminds me, in a flash of hug-memory, of when she said goodbye, and all the nervousness I felt at staying with Dad for so long. It feels so good to be wrapped in her arms.

"I was scared you were going to look all different. I feel like I've been here forever. You look the same. I'm so glad."

It's comforting to think I might be the same person I was, even if I can feel the changes grinding away. She steps back, out of the hug, and reaches out and takes my hand.

"How's she doing?" Dad asks. He puts his hand on

Mom's back. I hadn't thought about this, but I've heard that families come together when in crisis. You see it all the time in movies.

"She's improving. She's going to be fine. I kind of freaked out about all the blood she lost, but they say it often happens. It was just so hard to see her like that."

Dad has so much compassion in his eyes.

"They're saying she might be able to leave by next weekend. They're not sure if she'll go to a rehab place or home. She couldn't stay by herself yet at her house. I'll stay up here with her for a while either way, and see how she's doing, if that's okay."

"Of course," Dad says. "Marley can stay with me an extra week, or however long."

I walk over to the bed. I wish Grandma were awake, so we could talk. I wish she felt better, that she didn't look so much older than she did the last time I saw her, just a couple of months ago.

Still, seeing her, I feel something inside of me—something that is wound very, very tight—begin to relax a tiny bit. Somehow I knew this; I was right. I really did need to see her.

Mom sits back in the chair on the other side of the bed. "But she's really okay?" I don't know why I need to keep hearing her say it, but I do. Just like I had to come to see her in person.

Mom nods, her eyes looking into mine. My truth meter is locked in. She really is fine.

I grab the bag I packed for my mother and show her all the stuff I brought. When I pull out the plastic bottle of jasmine spray, she smiles at my father. "Thank you, Robert," she says. "That was really thoughtful."

Dad gets all awkward, silent.

My grandmother's eyes flutter a little, and then she opens them. She sees me and smiles, a sweet, slow smile. I take her hand and squeeze it.

"Hey, Grandma," I say. "It's so good to see you." It is. With her eyes open, I can see she's still her.

She smiles, a little loopy from sleep. "Marley Eden, honey," she says. I smile back, even though her speech is painfully slow. "Thank you for coming, sweetheart." Her hand is so warm, soft, just like it's always been. I squeeze it again, so relieved to be with her, to hear her voice. She squeezes my hand right back, weakly. She looks around the room a little until her eyes land on my dad. "And Robert. Thank you too. I'm glad to see you here."

He gives that awkward nod, but then smiles at her. Everyone loves Grandma.

She just looks at us for a while. We all smile at her, all three of us. She's only awake a little while. Most of that time she's smiling.

The relief is as palpable as a pillow, and I'm so thankful that we're all here together.

Giant Marley on the Screen

D ad gets lost on the way from the hospital to Yankee Stadium. He's not a get-lost kind of guy—he's too careful with maps and route planning to allow it to happen. But when he gets off the Major Deegan Expressway for a shortcut he took about a decade ago, we spend the next twenty-five minutes cruising the Bronx and testing out his cursing vocabulary. Eventually he finds a familiar road and gets me there.

"You have your cell phone in case you can't find Jack or you need me for any reason."

"I do. I'll be fine."

"It's my job to very nearly fall apart when I leave my daughter by herself at a ballpark in New York City."

"I won't be by myself." I grab my bag. "Don't expect me right after the game. Jack said his brother's going to take us out for dinner first."

"I remember. Have a great time. I'll be listening to the game on the way home, so don't try to run onto the field or anything."

"Yeah, that's so me. I'll see you, Dad." I shut the door and step out into the madness that surrounds Yankee Stadium.

It's pretty late—the game has already started—but there are still tons of people walking around the outside of the stadium. People walk fast, seem to know where they're headed. I follow the crowd into a gate, go through something like airport security, and then start looking for our seats. It's not as easy as it is in, say, a theater. This place has hundreds of levels and gates and sections, ramps and elevators and escalators, with people walking in every direction. I finally figure out where I need to be—out past the foul pole in left field. I walk up the small aisle, row D, E, F. There's Jack, sitting in row 10, seat 6.

"You made it," he says.

"I did."

"How's your grandmother?" He stands to let me by.

"Okay. Not like out-of-bed great, but she's going to be fine." I sit and look around. "Wow," I say.

I'd been to the old stadium when I was little, and I've seen the new one on TV a ton, but this is my first time here. It's hard to believe all these people—tens of thousands of people—are all here to watch nine guys play a game against nine other guys. The place is literally vibrating with excitement. People are stomping their feet, shouting at the pitcher, and all at once, everyone stands and starts clapping. I look at the scoreboard. There are two outs, and the count is three and two. The crowd is looking for a strikeout. Before I can even focus on the field, find the pitcher and home plate, the crowd erupts with cheers. The people in the rows ahead of us are all slapping high-fives. An inning-ending strikeout! Everyone sits back down.

Jack reaches beside him and hands me a hat. "I got you this." It's a Yankees hat, a newer version of the one my dad wears.

"You got me this?"

"You already have one?"

I laugh. "No, not at all. It's just, that was so nice of you. Thank you."

"You are like the perfect baseball hat girl," he says after I put it on my head.

"And by that you mean . . ?"

"Not everyone can pull off a baseball cap. Like puffy-haired people? They should not wear hats. But you have baseball hat hair."

"I'll work to view that as a compliment."

"It was meant as one," he says. My stomach: *flip, flip, flip*. So okay. He got me a hat. In some worlds, that might be perceived as a gesture of some kind. It's probably not fair to assume, though, that the Hadley family speaks the same language as mine. The Baird Family Language of the Gesture is complex and unique. The official ruling from the judges: a nice thing to do. Not necessarily loaded with emotional meaning.

"You want something to eat?" Jack asks.

"Not yet, thanks. What do you eat here?"

"Peanuts. Crackerjacks. Hot dogs. Baseball food."

"Mmm," I say. My stomach: *flip, flip, flip. NO!*

In the outfield, there's a screen where they show video of fans in the stands between innings. It's so funny to watch, because people suddenly see their faces up there, and then turn, as though to find the camera, but then they realize that when they're turned, duh, they can't see themselves on the screen anymore, and they turn back again really fast. Like a toddler trying to catch his shadow. I guess it depends on where you're sitting, because some people start jumping up and down, faces still forward, looking like they've won the lottery twice in a day. It's surprising to me that this isn't only true for little kids, but for older people too.

It's a great ball game. Every time the other team goes up a run, the Yankees come back in the bottom of the inning to tie it or go ahead again. The crowd is really into it. I'm having as much fun looking at all the people as Jack is watching the game.

There's a row of four guys in front of us, all wearing Yankees baseball caps in different shades of blue. The guy sitting in front of me sticks a red Coke bottle cap on top of the hat of the guy sitting in front of Jack. The other three just keep yukking it up, sneaking sideways glances, and slapping each other and their own legs when they realize it's still there. It's so stupid, but for some reason, Jack and I keep cracking up about it.

There are a lot of things, like stadium rituals, that everyone else seems to know instinctively. It's hard to get the knack of it, though. Like, everyone will start clapping that clap/clap, clap/clap/clap, clap/clap, clap/clap rhythm at once, and then repeat it, and then they'll all stop at once, while idiot me is still sort of clapping, and then looking around to see if anyone saw me clapping after everyone else had stopped. There's no pattern to it—sometimes they'll clap out the rhythm once, sometimes three times, or twice. Everyone around me seems to get it. Then there's me. *Clap, clap, clap. Oh.*

All these people—adults!—shout out players' names when they're at bat, cheering them on. They don't look even the tiniest bit self-conscious. Even Jack does this when his favorite player comes to bat.

I must be missing some basic genes. I can't pull off a patented Leah Stamnick Casual Arm Touch or Flirty Hair Flip. I can't look people in the eye when I meet them for the first time. And I most certainly cannot cheer out loud without feeling like the world's biggest idiot.

The guy in front of Jack pats his head—what makes him do that?—and finds the cap. He looks at his friends as though he wants to kill them, but in a good way.

The Yankees do it again in the bottom of the sixth—they're down by two, and then they go ahead by a run. The guy in front of Jack has another bottle cap on top of his hat. I didn't see them put it there, but there it is.

The seats are pretty close together here, and though I couldn't tell you a thing about the woman sitting to my left, I think I've memorized everything about the guy to my right. Jack's legs are pale and thin. They look especially thin in his baggy, dark blue shorts. He crosses one leg over the other, bouncing his black low-top Converse-clad foot in a slow, basic rhythm. The shoe-lace on his right sneaker is frayed. When he leans toward me, his clean almond smell rises above all the baseball smells, to my nose's great pleasure. In fact, all my senses are in a state of heightened, deeply contented aware-ness. I want him to reach out for my hand, or casually put his arm around me. He doesn't. I could just grab his hand, but what if I'm just his good old *Marley-and-Me*-dog-movie baseball-loving neighbor-friend?

After the third out in the inning, there's a commo-tion to the right of us, and I see that the man on the outfield screen is actually sitting two sections away. He's dancing this awful hip-shaking dance (and he has very ample hips to shake), and I see his daughter, about my age, sinking down in her seat, leaning all the way to the left, to try to stay off the screen. Finally, she just stands up and walks away.

There are some really lame fathers in this world.

And some really bratty daughters.

I look away from the real dad to watch the dad on the screen, but the camera's panning now, and there's something familiar up there. It's my shirt. It's me. It's me and Jack. On the giant screen in the outfield of

Yankee Stadium. Yes, of course. Why not? What next? Jack grins, looking at the screen, not me. I just stare, because that giant girl up there looks so different from how I think of myself. Look at her in her new Yankees hat! She looks perfectly comfortable. At ease. Happy and relaxed. Here at Yankee Stadium with one fine-looking guy.

And then the camera slides back to our right, where that dad, the big-bellied one, is still doing his hip-rolling boogie.

"Wow," Jack says.

"Amen," I say.

"You want to walk around a little?"

"Sure."

We go downstairs, where there are concession stands and carts selling everything from hot dogs to blender drinks and beer and cotton candy. "What can I get you?" he asks.

"Not hungry," I say.

"You will eat," he says.

"Aren't we going out with your brother? I'll just eat then."

"You're always supposed to eat at a ballpark."

"I see your point." I buy us two pretzels and a Coke, trying not to think about the fact that it costs nearly a day's worth of my twin-watching salary. "Mustard?" I ask.

"On a pretzel?" he says.

"Some people do."

"Not this people."

"Yeah, me neither."

We go back to our seats and watch the rest of the game. At one point, Jack leans forward and puts a soda bottle cap on the head of the guy in front of him. The guy feels it immediately, and turns to give his friends some grief. Then he turns around to Jack with a big laughing smile.

I just sit back and take in the baseball scene, glad I never said anything to Jack about maybe not being such a big Yankees fan. Because I like this. I really do. It's not just sitting next to Jack. It's the whole thing, this place where everyone's sitting together in their little groups, but also part of a big, 50,000-person crowd.

I keep thinking about the giant Marley on the screen. I'm so glad I saw her. She looks like she's doing great.

Just Another Loser Kid

I have never in all my thirteen years been in a crowd as thick as this one. I wouldn't have described myself as the claustrophobic type, but as we move along, carried by the masses, I long to rise above it and walk on everyone's shoulders. To pull in a deep breath of fresh air. I'm crammed on all sides. I concentrate on staying next to Jack and breathing.

Once we're out of the gate and we round the side of the stadium, a lot of people head to the subway and the crowd thins a bit. Jack points with his chin at the McDonald's across the street. I nod.

We walk around the outside of the building and then check inside. Dean's not there yet. Jack grabs us some fries and we sit on the concrete outside and watch the people leaving the stadium. There are all these little boys in their Yankees shirts, each with a player's name and number on the back. "I think my dad always wanted a son. A little Yankees boy, you know?"

"Why do you think that?"

"He doesn't exactly get me. The things he likes to do are all just boy things. It's like we don't have a single common interest."

"Well, I'm glad you're not a boy."

I hate to quote Leah, even in my own head, but OH! My God!

Jack stands up—is his face flushed red? He peers down the street both ways, then sits down again.

"You want to call him?"

"He's probably just stuck in traffic. It's hard to get here when a game lets out. I hope you don't mind just hanging a bit. He'll get through eventually. What time is it?"

I pull out my cell phone. "Ten to five," I say. "What time did he say he'd be here?"

"Four thirty."

The streets are clogged with cars trying to get out of parking lots, lined up to get on the highway.

"Yeah. Let me give him a call."

He dials a number and waits, then hangs up. "I didn't even get voice mail. I don't know—sometimes he doesn't pay his bill. He might not even have service right now."

"Do you want to call your parents and see if he left a message?"

"Nah, I don't want to freak them out. Let's give it a little longer."

So we sit there, talking about nothing and everything. But it gets later and later, and I can see him growing quieter, more upset, angry-looking.

"You want a soda?" I ask. "I'm going in for a Diet Coke."

"No, thanks."

Inside I use the bathroom, taking a quick look in the mirror. It must be the hat, but I really look like some other person, a smaller version of Marley on the Screen. When I come outside again, Jack's holding his phone, looking even more pissed.

"Did you call anyone?"

"Yeah. I just called my parents to tell them I'd be

later than I said. I didn't mention anything about Dean not being here, but they didn't say anything either. Listen, I don't want you to freak out your dad, but do you think you should call him?"

Ugh. I guess I have to. I'd rather not. He was so nervous about me being here. I can't just not come home when he expects me. I call, but he's not home. Where is he? Over at the Krolls'? I just hang up.

"So what do we do?" I ask.

"I don't think waiting is going to do it," Jack says. "I'm really sorry. He can be such a . . ."

"No, listen. I had a great day. I would have come even if I'd known there was no dinner and no Dean to take us home. Should we just take the train or something?"

"Do you think your father might flip out?"

"Yeah. Let me try him again." I call, no answer. I leave a message this time, telling him what's going on, that we're taking the train, around when I expect to be home. I also mention that he might want to think about entering the millennium we live in and invest in a cell phone all his own.

"I'm sorry about all this. I'm so pissed. I can't believe he stranded us in the Bronx. Dean is such a total—"

"It's totally fine. I've never been on the subway. It'll—"

"Shut UP!"

"Excuse me?" I'm startled, but he said it in a friendly way.

"You've literally never been on the subway? Did you grow up in some foreign kingdom?"

"Maybe I did. Maybe I didn't."

He smiles. We cross the street and he leads me through the turnstile, using his MetroCard to pay for my entry. We only have to wait about five minutes before a train comes. It's crowded but not full, so we share a seat near the door.

I'm just looking around, taking it all in, the little signs, the freaky people, the hyperhip New York people, when, of all things, my cell phone rings.

"You're okay?"

"Fine, Dad. Really. Where were you?"

"Out getting a cell phone."

"Oh my God, really?

"No, but that would be funny, wouldn't it?"

"Your kind of funny. Are you freaked out?"

"Do you want me to come and get you? Where are you now?"

"We're already on our way home. I'm on the subway. We'll catch a train home out of Penn Station."

"Are you sure you're going to be okay?"

"What happened to 'Nothing like the train'?"

"When you know which train you're on, give me a call. I'll pick you up at the station. Jack's with you, right?"

"Yeah, why?"

"I just feel better knowing that you're not alone."

"Okay. I'll call you. Bye."

"Is he pissed?" Jack asks.

"No, but I got the distinct impression he might have been if you weren't here with me."

"What do you mean? Here, we get off at the next stop." We stand and hold on to the rail by the door as the subway's brakes screech us to a jolting stop.

As we wait for the next train, I have some time to figure out why my dad's concern bothers me. "He didn't seem at all worried when you took the train here by yourself. He just doesn't know what to do with a girl. A daughter. It's like I'm foreign. Like, that night Leah was over. He felt so out of place with all that girl talk and girl stuff in the house that he ran outside."

"I don't know, Marley. Maybe he was trying to do a nice thing, give you some privacy. Like he didn't want you to feel he was on top of you guys or anything."

Here we go again: Jack is on my father's side. I should make it a practice not to talk to my father about

Jack and not to talk to Jack about my father. Something about hearing each one talk about the other really gives me the willies.

As we take train after train to Penn Station, our talk finds its way back to our families. At one point, when he's talking about Dean, he gets totally angry, red-in-the-face mad and then he looks at me and shuts down.

"What?" I ask him. "What is it?"

"I just hate that my brother's so screwed up, that he left us like that. It's not the first time he's screwed up and it's just . . . embarrassing. Like, Will's family was just normal and yours is normal and I have this brother who's constantly—"

"Hello? Jack? What normal family? How many parents live in my house? How many live in yours? I'm just another loser kid whose parents aren't together. I know there's nothing unique about it, but it's really not normal."

Jack nods. "Well, I'm sorry that I have a total jerkoff brother who makes promises and doesn't keep them. It's one thing when he screws up and messes with my plans—but I'm just so pissed that he let you down too. I hate that when someone in your family screws up; it's not like you can just walk away. I'm stuck with my family. I'm really sorry for how tonight turned out."

"I'm not," I say. I mean it. And I think about how Jack's family doesn't seem perfect to him, even though both parents are there. Even though they live in one home and he's not constantly shuttling back and forth. I wonder if anyone's family feels perfect. Mine was for a long time. And I didn't even know it.

When we finally reach Penn Station, we walk its long, grand hallways. There are groups of kids a little older than us, with big backpacks, leaning against the wall. I'll bet their fathers aren't waiting at home, watching the clock until it's time to meet them at a train.

Jack guides me to a long line. "I've got this." He buys my ticket and hands it to me.

We ride the train, and mostly just relive the day. At one point he puts a soda bottle cap on my head and waits for me to notice.

When we get off the train, Dad's there to take us home. We say good night in front of my house, and I watch as Jack walks by the stacks of deteriorating cartons that contain my dad's old life, still piled up at the curb.

Not Easy to Be Brave

∞

It rains most of the next week, and the twins and I are going more and more bonkers each day. We watch every Disney video at least three times. I swat away little cartoon bluebirds that seem to circle my head.

When the sun shines Thursday morning, I'm so grateful, I feel like shouting praises up toward heaven. Lynne helps me make a picnic lunch for the girls, and we pack it, along with their training-wheeled bikes, into the car.

"I do not need training wheels," Faith says.

"We know, Faith," Lynne says.

"Well, kwee just bring that tool that takes them off so I can just try? I just want to try."

Lynne looks at Grace.

"I could try too."

"Are you ready?"

"I don't know. I could try."

Lynne shows me how to take off the training wheels. "I'll put a screwdriver in the cooler and you should have no problem." She reaches into her trunk and pulls out a white case with a red cross on the front. "Take this first-aid kit just in case," she says.

On the bike path at the park, the girls ride with their training wheels on for less than a minute before Faith is begging me to take the wheels off.

"Mine too!" Grace says.

"I can't teach you both at once. We're going to have to take turns." I have an image of the first time I did this, my dad holding on to the back of my bike, running along with me. This is one of those things you're supposed to do with your father. Or at least your mother. Why hasn't their mother taught them? Poor Faith and Grace are stuck with me.

There must be a right way to do this. "Listen," I say. "I'm only going to take them off one bike. You guys are both sharing both bikes."

"We don't share good," Faith says.

"If you want to learn this today, you have to share well."

"You mean we both ride each other's bikes sometimes?" Grace asks.

"Exactly."

"That's okay with me," Grace says.

"Well, not me," Faith says.

"I'm going to take the training wheels off one bike. Grace's bike. Your bike will still have training wheels. If you want to learn to ride a two-wheeler today, it's going to be on Grace's bike. Then, when I'm teaching Grace, you can ride your own bike, which will have training wheels on it."

Faith walks into the playground and marches up a wooden seesaw. She stands in the middle, seeking balance, one foot on each side. Then she sits.

"What's she doing, Marley?" Grace asks as I start to take the training wheels off her bike.

"Thinking."

Faith comes running back. "Okay," she says.

"Okay," I say.

"Okay," Grace says. They stand there as I struggle with the screwdriver and training wheels.

Finally! "Let's go," I say.

Grace rides Faith's bike and I walk the two-wheeler over to the bike path. I check to be sure Faith's helmet is on the right way. It is. "Climb aboard," I say.

She does.

"Okay, Faith," I say, stalling for time. "Wait, Grace, you ride ahead a little bit, so you guys don't get in each other's way. Okay. Good. Now, Faith, here's what we're going to do. I'll hold on to the back of your bike, and maybe the handlebars too, and you're going to ride. You need to look straight ahead, not right down at the path, and you need to pedal, and not freak out."

"Marley, I can do it. Don't hold on. I can do it by myself."

"No, I need to—"

And she takes off before I can finish. She wobbles then straightens and then tumbles in a heap to the ground, her bike on top of her. She wails. It takes all of two seconds for her to go from riding to tumbling to screaming and crying. Grace climbs off her bike and beats me to Faith by a second.

I pull the bicycle off Faith and pull her up to a sitting position. "Are you okay?"

"Nooooooo!!!"

"What hurts?"

Faith looks at me, and I realize it's the first time I've seen her cry. It has always been Grace. "I hurt my knee! I hurt my—It's BLEEDING! Marley, my knee is bleeding!"

"It's okay, Faith. We'll put a bandage on it and it'll be fine. Don't freak out."

I remember some things from being five, and one of them is that as soon as I saw that blood was dripping, I'd freak out. Fast bandage application is essential. "Grace, can you get me that backpack, please?" She races over to the bench and brings it to me. "Okay. Here's the first-aid kit. I'm going to just clean out—"

"No clean out! That stings! No way. NO!"

"Let me just see what . . ." I look through the box, but all that's there are wipes and bandages.

"We need to clean it, Faith, or it can get all disgusting and infected, and—"

"Nooooo!" she shrieks.

"Are you okay?" Jack. Jack's voice. Jack?

"Marley, it's your brother," Grace says.

"Brother Jack, at your service," he says. "Can I see your knee?" he asks Faith. She's still crying hard.

"No wipes!" she screams. "No sting wipes!"

"I don't like sting wipes either," Jack says.

"Me too," Faith says. She's still crying, but not as hard.

In a stage whisper he asks me, "Did you tell them I was your brother?"

I widen my eyes with a held-in grin. "Um, no."

He's reaching around inside his gym bag, opening something and pouring it. "Here. This," he says, "is water. It is not a stinging wipe. It is water on a paper towel." He hands it to me. I put it on her knee before she can object. "Marley's just going to put it on your knee for a second."

She nods, a sad little nod of acceptance.

"How'd you know she was hurt?" I ask.

"We all heard her scream," Jack says. "I think people in South America may have heard her scream."

Faith smiles, a tiny bit, and says, "I scream good."

"Definitely," Jack says.

"I could sort of see you too. I was behind the backstop, chasing fouled-off balls."

"Thank you so much."

He bows and takes a step backwards. "My great pleasure."

"Bye, Marley's brother," Grace says.

"Bye, Marley's brother," Faith says. "Thanks for not letting Marley sting my leg."

"See you later," I say.

He nods.

"Well, that was fun," I say.

"I'm ready," Grace says.

"For lunch?"

"My turn."

"To what?"

"To ride the bike with no training wheels."

"But," I start. Then I shut up. Because it's not easy to be brave, and she's being so brave. Not stupid. Just brave. Apparently there's a clear difference sometimes.

"Okay," I say, starting over. "Let's first eat a little snack so Faith's knee can get used to its new bandage and we can get some good riding energy here. After we've had a snack, it's your turn. Deal?"

"Deal. Hey, Marley?" Grace is tugging on my shorts.

"Yeah?"

"Knock, knock."

"Who's there?"

"Jack."

"Jack who?"

"Jack your brother!" Faith screams as she races to the bench.

"It's my joke!" Grace shouts after her.

"Jack who, Grace?" I say.

"Not Jack Whograce. Jack Who."

"Jack who?"

"Jack, a thin man just walked by." She smiles, proud.

"Good one." I smile back.

We sit on the benches, and I take out cookies and juice packs for all three of us. Faith has returned to her usual self. She's trying to take one of Grace's cookies, but Grace is having none of it. She wants to eat and get up on that bicycle.

"I'm ready, Marley."

"I need a couple more minutes, Grace. Just a few more. Hey, Faith, are you going to sit here while Grace practices or do you want to ride your bike?"

"I'll ride." She bites her cookie in half, then shoves the other half right in her mouth behind the first. "It's hard, you know, Grace. You're gonna fall and get hurt."

"Marley's brother'll help me."

"He's not my brother."

"Okay, your cousin."

"What? No. But *I'll* help you."

"'Kay. Thanks."

"Here's what we're going to do," I tell Grace as she climbs on the bike. "Let me see if your feet touch the ground. Good. Now you're going to sort of just scoot forward with your feet on the ground, and when you get going a little bit, put your feet on the pedals and start pedaling."

"Okay." She sits there for a while.

"Are you ready?"

"I'm ready in my head. I'm just scared to start."

"I know how that feels," I say. "But let's do it."

"Be careful, Grace," Faith says. "Just be careful."

"I'm ready." And we set off, slowly. It's hard to balance when you go slowly, so I start to push the bike a little. "Put your feet on the pedals," I say. "I'm hold-ing on."

"I'm scared."

"I know," I say. "But I'm helping. Come on, I'll run with you. Just push, pedal!"

And she does. She begins to pedal, and she wobbles sharply, the bike almost falling. I hold on tight and help her straighten out the handlebars.

"Look straight ahead," I tell her, still holding on, running alongside, trying to help her hold her balance.

"Okay," she yells. "I'm scared."

And then I trip. I just go down right on my knee,

feel the skin scrape. I scramble to my feet and chase after the bike, after Grace, but she's doing it, her little legs
pumping hard. She's slowly wobbling her way down the
path. By herself.

"Go, Grace!" Faith says.

She gets steadier as she goes.

"Stop now, Grace," I yell. She slows down, then
puts her feet down. She steps off the bike, lays it on the
grass alongside the path, and then starts jumping up
and down, her arms over her head.

Faith comes over and asks, "Could I try again? It's
Grace's bike and so I wasn't used to it but I could now.
Could I? Now?"

"Of course. You'll get it this time. You're so close.
Great job, Grace. You were awesome."

Before long, the training wheels are off both bikes.
Faith and Grace are wobbling down the path on two
wheels by themselves.

* * *

I can tell the storm is coming from the way the trees
look. Branches are blowing; leaves look more silver than
green, twisting in the wind, blowing upside down, then
back. Gray clouds roll in and darken the sky with the

kind of quiet stillness that fills a theater the instant before a show starts.

And it is then that I see Leah's pink and yellow bike
snaking its way along the path. She's probably on her way
home from flirting with Jack at the baseball field, racing to
beat the storm. I start to sing under my breath that song
from *The Wizard of Oz,* the one that plays as the evil
Miss Gulch comes to take away Dorothy's beloved Toto.
Dunt da-dunt da DA da, dunt da-dunt da DA da!

She pulls up in front of me. "Hey, Marley."

"I'm Grace." She smiles sweetly at Leah.

"Are you Marley's friend?" Faith asks.

That was once the million-dollar question. It took
some time, some painful time, but I finally know the
answer. I do not like Leah. I do not trust her. And I'm
going to try to do the right thing.

Leah ignores Faith. "So what are you up to?" she
asks me. "Do you want to hang out or something?"

I think about Rig, how he kept walking by Beulah's
house long after she was gone, still looking for his friend.
Long after his friend was already gone. The rain begins
to come down, and the drops are heavy, as if the rain's
been waiting a long time to fall, the drops growing fatter
all the time.

It's too hard to say *Our friendship is over* or even *We're done,* so I use the words she and Jane kept saying to me, "I'm pretty busy, Leah."

Being alone in school will be really hard; it's almost impossible to think about. But being with Leah is even harder.

"Busy like for weeks busy? Come on, Marley. I'm sorry, okay? I'll be a better friend. Let's just get over it, okay?"

All those days of friendship add up to something big, something impossible to erase. Something that has come to its natural, if not altogether peaceful, end. I don't know how to say that, though.

Leah jumps on the silence like it's an opportunity. "Come on, Marley. Let's just hang and get back to normal. I've really missed you."

"I don't know, Leah. I think it's just time." As in *not enough time.* Also: *it's time.* People change, move on. We're not what we were. *And I do not trust you at all.*

"Ugh," Leah says with a new variety of hair flip— the Leah Stamnick Hair Flip of Disgust and Frustration. "I wish I hadn't signed up for Curtain Call. It's so not what I thought it would be." I recognize something in her voice, and in her face. There's that about-to-cry-any-minute feeling that tormented me for months. It sucks to feel miserable. It's hard to see Leah like this.

My brain keeps flashing images of second-grade Leah smiling at me with the love of pure friendship. Part of me wants to hug her. Just not the part in charge of actual body movements.

I hear the distant sound of rumbling thunder, the kind that tells sensible people to wrap up what they're doing and head indoors.

"You know what? Their mother is going to be here soon. Come on, Grace, Faith. Let's go wait for your mom in the parking lot."

"You're just leaving?"

"Yeah, we have to go."

"Well, let me know when you want to get together," she says.

Is there any way to end a friendship without having to say something painful? "Really, I'm just busy, Leah." Why can't I find better words?

"What kind of busy could you really just be? Busy with some stupid baseball guy or busy sulking and being depressed? You're not the first person whose parents got divorced. People still have fun with their friends. Jane was sick of you a long time ago, but I kept waiting for you to pull it together, get back to how you used to be—"

"Don't bother, Leah. Really. Come on, let's go," I say to the twins.

"Marley Bear," Faith says. "We don't care if we get wet. You could stay here. With your friend."

"She's pretty," Grace says.

"We're going now," I say.

"Marley Bear, why don't you want to stay with your friend?"

I want to tell Faith to be quiet, but I think she really wants an answer. She must want a lot of answers. She has to be wondering why her father isn't around anymore. Why did this person who was part of her life disappear? And will that keep happening to her?

"Tell her, *Marley Bear*," Leah says, her voice hard and mean. "I'd like to hear you put a good spin on it."

"Goodbye, Leah," I say. Simply and clearly. Just like that.

I go to grab the bikes, and the rain starts to come down very hard. We head to the parking lot. We don't bother running, as we're soaked through almost instantaneously. "That girl was my friend once," I tell Faith and Grace. "People change, and sometimes friends grow apart." I stop. Oh my God. I'm reciting my father's separation speech. I try to find a truer way to explain.

"Basically, your friends are supposed to be nice and good to you," I say. "That girl wasn't."

"I just like fun friends," Faith says. She runs away from me to jump into a puddle, and then runs back.

Grace is lagging behind. I stop to let her catch up and she reaches for my hand and squeezes it.

I don't see Lynne's minivan in the parking lot, but Dad's truck is there. I take the twins over and load them into the cab. My dad helps them with their seat belts. "I was cutting grass down the street and thought I'd see if you were here," he says. "Want to see if Jack wants a ride?"

I nod. "I need to get their bikes and some other stuff." I start running toward the baseball field. One other person is running in the same direction. When we get to the field, I see Jack jumping from puddle to puddle with a little kid. When the kid sees the person running next to me, he screams, "Dad!" and starts running toward him. Jack turns to reach for his bag, then looks back and sees me.

"We'll give you a ride!" I shout.

He nods and jogs over to where I am. "Where are the twins?"

"My dad's truck."

We run toward the bike path, Jack a little ahead of

me. I slip on the grass (grateful that he didn't have a clear view of it) and fall on my butt. I slip again as I try to stand. Can I not ever in my life have one moment when I don't look like a complete fool? Jack turns around and reaches out his hand for me. He pulls me up, and keeps my hand in his all the way to the path where the twins' bikes are sprawled.

He grabs Faith's and I take Grace's, along with the first-aid kit, training wheels, and the cooler. We race over to Dad's truck and load everything in the back.

We drive to the Krolls'. She brings out two umbrellas and I help her walk the girls inside.

"Should I help you get them into dry clothes?" I ask. I want to leave, but two wet, hyper girls and a baby is a lot for anyone to handle. Even a grating-voiced anyone.

"That's okay, Marley. Your dad is waiting. I'm going to just give the girls a bath now anyway. Jenna's sleeping. It's fine. We'll see you tomorrow, okay?"

"Okay. Did they tell you how well they rode?"

"Mom! You have to see us! We're great! We rocked!" Faith follows Lynne to the stairs.

"Hey, Marley?" Grace says.

"Yeah, Grace?"

"Thanks." She walks over and hugs me. "Bye, Marley Bear."

Brave as I'll Ever Be

∞

Dad stops in front of Jack's house to let him out. There's an old-looking black car in the driveway. "Dean's here," Jack says. "You want to meet him?"

"Sure," I say, not sure if this is the truth, but thinking there's no other acceptable answer. "Let me just change."

I run into the house and pull the soaked clothes off my body. I pull on the Yankees shirt my dad gave me all those weeks ago and shorts, and find an umbrella in my dad's closet. Wait. Ugh. Drowned-rat hair. No time. No choice. Ponytail.

I'm excited to finally have a chance to see the inside of Jack's house, maybe get a look at his parents. That's not happening today, as Dean is sitting on the porch, out of the rain, right next to Jack.

"You must be—"

"Marley," Jack says. "She lives in Will's old house."

"Well, my dad does," I say. "And I'm staying here with him."

Dean looks nothing like Jack. I was hoping for a glimpse of something, that way siblings' qualities sometimes echo each other in interesting ways. That is not the case here. Dean has a gross, thin mustache and a cigarette tucked over his left ear.

"Were you the one with Jack at the game?"

"Yup. It was a great game."

"I'm sorry I left you stranded there. I just got kind of tied up."

"Oh, it was fine. We made it home."

"No thanks to you," Jack says.

Dean just rolls his eyes at Jack and then turns back to me. "I owe you dinner. Come out with Jack and me sometime?"

"That sounds great," I say. "It was nice to meet you, but I need to go dry off."

We say goodbye and I start to walk away.

"Oh," I say, remembering that Jack's dog lives with Dean now. "Is Scout with you?"

Dean turns to Jack. "You told her about Scout?"

"Yeah. You should meet her dog. He's named after Lou Gehrig."

"Cool," Dean says. "Scout's not here tonight. Next time, okay, Marley?"

"Sure," I say, taking a moment of pleasure in realizing that this was a perfectly normal, not forced and awkward, first conversation with a stranger.

Going up the back stairs, I almost trip over a potted plant. It wasn't there yesterday. I take a closer look. It's a small plant; I'd know it anywhere from the long, spatula-shaped, notched leaves and the small buds close to the soil. A dandelion, potted in a planter by my weed-hating dad. This could only be a gesture. It must have killed him to do it—to rescue a plant he'd want to exterminate, and plant it. For me.

I go inside and take a shower.

I let the thoughts just run loose in my brain instead of trying to hold them all inside. And I wait for wisdom.

Wisdom's a no-show.

But I do know some things. I don't get to choose how I feel; you can't be a nursery school director's daughter without learning those basics. I could recite it all:

There are no bad feelings, just bad actions. Treat others the way you want to be treated yourself. The thing is, those rules overlook one basic fact: Really hard, horrible things happen even when you've been on your best behavior. And I guess there is no manual to help you through it. Life is about figuring it all out.

But I have learned something this summer. Life has some fantastic surprises too. And some of them have amazing light blue eyes.

* * *

I get dressed and look around the room. It hasn't changed since my first day here. I find a small table in the garage and place it next to the bed. I take a light from the dresser and put it on the table for nighttime reading. When I come next time, maybe I'll put some pictures on the wall.

Later, I go into the kitchen and sit at the table, next to my dad. In our family language, you don't directly acknowledge gestures. But maybe it's time for some changes. "I saw that dandelion plant," I say.

He smiles. "I dug it out of the Martinezes' lawn, but then I had to hide out in my truck while I planted it. I have a reputation to uphold."

"Because you'd look so nice and normal if someone spotted you potting a dandelion plant in your truck."

Dad grins at me.

"I decided to use some of my babysitting money to pay for your Internet connection once school starts. Once your computer's fixed."

"That's really nice of you, Marley. I don't think it'll be neces—"

"I want to," I say.

"Okay," Dad says. "Thank you." He keeps staring at the coffee-cup clock. "Can I talk to you a minute?"

"Can I just say no?"

"Not really. I have to get this over with."

I don't want to go through all this again. To hear how it's no one's fault. Or how I should learn from Babe Ruth and other Yankees greats.

"I don't know how to frame this one, Marley. You know I'm not good at this kind of thing, so I'm going to just say it. Your mother and I are going to get a divorce. It won't be ugly or anything like that—we're going to work it out peacefully, and we expect to always be friends."

I expect to feel it in my gut, like an unexpected kick. I don't. There's nothing. It's possible I already knew. Or maybe it's just not that different from how things already are, except that the nagging hope is gone. It's sort of sad, though, that giving up hope could make me feel better. Maybe the hope that was there has already been pushed into another spot. Like the way I can look ahead to school and think about maybe sitting at lunch with Callie instead of by myself. Or looking ahead another year, when Jack and I will go to the same high school.

"It'll be a lot like it's been the past few months, only I'm going to stay in this house; I won't keep moving around."

I look out the back door, toward Jack's backyard. The rain is blowing hard, slanted. "And Lynne?"

"What about her?"

"Is she . . . are you . . . What's the deal?"

"We've been helping each other get through a really difficult time. I'm not sure you realize that you've been helping me a lot too. I love having you here. Really. I never pictured there being any genuine up-side to being in this situation, but I think it'll give us a chance to get to know each other in a different way, a meaningful one. Spending this time with you, just us—it's really been special to me."

"You don't expect me to call this a wonderful turn of events, right? You'll forgive me for not finding the bright side."

"I will," he says. "I'll forgive you anything."

I think I knew that. It's still nice to hear. "Anything?"

He nods, serious. "Yes."

"Like any disappointment, anything? Because I think there's something you should know."

He gets a look on his face like he's scared I'm going to mention that I've signed on to join a cult of dandelion-worshiping zealots.

"I haven't been completely honest."

"Just say it, Marley."

I'm enjoying this, even though he looks pained. Or maybe because he looks pained. "I've let you believe something that isn't quite true."

"Say it *now*." A cult of dandelion-worshiping, Yankees-hating zealots.

"I don't like fishing."

He sits back in his chair with a big sigh. "Really?"

"Yeah. I can't stand it. I'd rather, like, learn how to play ice hockey or audition for the rodeo or something."

"I can live with that." The sky brightens with lightning, and then there's a crash of thunder as it goes dark again. "So is this your way of telling me that you want to play ice hockey?"

"Not exactly. I think I'll actually just read awhile and go to bed early. If I can sleep through this storm."

"You know what all this rain means, right?"

"Uh, puddles?"

"The grass will grow. I, Robert T. Baird, shall cut it back down."

"Dandelions will grow too," I say.

"You say it like it's a good thing."

"I do."

He kisses my forehead. I go to my room. I climb into bed, savoring the feel of clean sheets against clean skin. I fall asleep to the sound of steady rain.

* * *

In the early morning's slanted light, the grass is still soaked from last night's storm. I roam the backyard, thinking that I should go inside and read, or sit and watch TV, but my legs seem to need to keep moving, so I just keep walking around. The soppy ground slushes beneath my shoes. I can feel the wet weight as the bottoms of my pants grow damp, then soaked, saturated.

In the far corner, back by Jack's yard, something white, dirty white, is sticking up at an odd angle beneath the maple tree. Rig seems to spot it at the same time I do, and he trots over and begins to sniff it. I bend and peek around him. It's a box, a falling-apart-from-being-wet white box. The old Monopoly box. Right next to it, lying together in a small, dirty silver lump, are two Monopoly pieces—the hat and the shoe.

I pick up the box and look beneath it. Nothing. I leave the box and pieces where they are. I walk all over the backyard, Rig trotting patiently beside me. I search all over the grass, behind the shrubs, in the flower bed. Nothing. I walk over the length of the lawn, from the street to the tree and back again. I start to look in places it could never be—in the middle of a tall hedge, on the low branch of a tree. I don't really know why I care—we have a whole new game, and it's not like Leah and Jane and I are ever going to play again. I just have to know where that dog piece ends up, if that dog's okay.

"Hey, did you will me out?" Jack asks. I didn't hear him come outside, or walk over, but he's standing right behind me.

"Not this time," I say. I suck at willing. Luckily, Jack always seems to show up eventually anyway.

"What are you looking for?"

"A dog."

Jack points at Rig and Rig makes a monkey sound

in delight, thinking Jack is about to play with him. "That was easy. Next?"

"Har," I say, and elbow him in the stomach. "A Monopoly dog," I reach inside some of the little holes where the dandelion plants used to grow. Not in there.

Jack shoves his hands into his pockets. He pulls out a fist and puts it right in front of my nose, then opens his fingers slowly. There, in the middle of his palm, is the little silver Monopoly dog.

"I didn't know you were looking for it," he says. "I found it last night."

I think about that. He saw it. He picked it up. He took it home. This morning, it found its way into his pocket again. He didn't pick up the hat or the shoe, just the dog. You'd have to classify that as a Jack Hadley Gesture.

He takes my hand in his and puts the dog right in the center of my palm. He folds my fingers gently around it, then even more gently wraps his fingers around mine.

It is not easy to be brave. It takes courage to act. Jack is holding my hand and looking right into my eyes. I free my hand and place the dog back in his. He sort of nods, and while his chin is down, close to me, I call on some courage buried deep within and lean forward, brave as

I'll ever be. Of course, my lips end up grazing his cheek, and I'm thinking that we have to find a way past this cheek thing. In that same instant, he turns his head, his lips seeking mine. Hoooo boy, do they find them.

Rig tries to walk between us. I feel him pushing through our legs, beating his thump thump thump tail against my leg. I soon forget, as I am wholly focused on a slightly more interesting activity.

* * *

Miracles are occurring.

All the twins want to do, all day long, is ride their bikes. They listen when I tell them it's time for lunch. They do not fight. They do not whine. They ride their bikes and eat their lunch and that is all.

But the bigger news, the truer miracle, is the fact of what my lips and Jack's lips did this morning. Though it didn't last long, I think about it so much I can almost feel that kiss again. I can't wait for the next lip-miracle.

After work, Dad drives past the hideous remains of his cartons for the hundredth time. And standing right next to them, a waving-at-us Jack. Before we even pull into the driveway, I have a plan.

I follow Dad into the house and then run back

out and over to Jack with an armful of black trash bags.

"What a thoughtful gift," he says. And then kisses me.

Kisses me!

Is this my life now? Every time I appear I get kissed by Jack?

I like.

Together, we start packing up all the trash into bags.

Dad sticks his head out the back door. "What are you doing?"

"Let's take all this to the dump," I say, looking around at the Monopoly remnants, at Dad's papers, the soggy cardboard boxes that contain his old life. And parts of mine too. "I don't think a bulk trash truck's ever going to show up."

He nods. "Throw the bags in the truck and we'll go. You coming, Jack?"

I'm so sure Jack wants to spend his time sandwiched in the front of my dad's truck with a huge haul of trash in the back.

Jack takes my hand and squeezes it. "Wouldn't miss it," he says.

* * *

I've never been to a garbage dump, but I like to picture it as a vast and surprisingly unsmelly place that spreads out with infinite horizons. *(What? Dumps can be unsmelly in fantasies.)*

A place where you stand in the back of your truck and get rid of your past, the broken parts of your past, anyway. The parts you no longer need. You throw it all away, two-handed, box after box. Just hurl it off the back of the truck. One thing, another, more! Goodbye!

Watch it all rain down on the not-at-all-smelly dump.

Just leave it there. Drive away.

Maybe it's the one place in this world where when you make the hard decision to get rid of something, it doesn't keep showing up. On its pink and yellow bike, just for example.

It doesn't hurt if there's a guy with light blue eyes in that truck, waiting to sit right next to you. To take your hand and rub his fingers softly over yours. To sometimes bring your hand to his mouth for a sweet and gentle kiss.

(For the record: that part is not a fantasy. It is amazingly, fantastically real.)

THE END

My mother, Judy Glassman, must be singled out. She was a wise, kind, and funny book-loving woman. I miss her every day.

Love and thanks to Jules and Barbara Glassman: staunch supporters, proud readers, and, I suspect, secret book salesmen. My sisters, Beth Arnold and Ellen Gidaro, are my foundation. For two so wee, they are crazy strong.

Mega thanks to Olugbemisola Amusashonubi-Perkovich, whose friendship is one of the great gifts of my adult life; Kim Marcus, my first-novel writing friend, who has a great eye and a great heart; Dorothy Crane, whose friendship and unwavering affinity for this book have always touched my heart.

Enormous gratitude to those who unwittingly inspired me: Laura Ruby, who has no idea that she taught me how to write a novel; Jeff Melnick, for a conversation about why writing matters even before the first sale; Patti Gauch, an extraordinary teacher, editor, and cheerleader, for making me really want to write a novel; and Esmeralda Santiago, Amy Hill Hearth, and David Wroblewski, real writers who treated me like I was one too.

Shout out to Holly Lemanowicz, my first (then) teen reader.

Two incredibly supportive groups, the Atomic Engineers and the Gango, have provided grand companionship on the bumpy road. The New Jersey State Council on the Arts honored an early version of this novel with a fiction fellowship; I will always be grateful.

A barrel of mojitos for Erin Murphy for having a good feeling when this manuscript went out into the world, and for seven million other things (NS).

My thanks to everyone at Clarion Books for the solid support and the deeply appreciated show of faith in a debut novelist, particularly Jennifer Greene, an editor with just the right touch and a very generous soul, even if she does favor the wrong season.

Big, back-slapping hugs to all my family and friends who celebrate each incremental achievement as though I single-handedly developed the alphabet, especially Aunt Eleanor, Karen Ravn, Tara Michaels, Abby Parigian, Sudipta Bardhan-Quallen, Pamela Ross, Lisa Mullarkey, and Karen Beson.

I end with love and thanks (and a Danish basket or two) for Michael, Jacob, and Anna, for allowing me to disappear to write and for the kind of unwavering support and pride that powers a creative life. I'm grateful that you've made our home a place filled with wise, kind, and funny book-loving people. It's my favorite place to be.